'Simone, don't!

She tensed. 'Don't v

'Don't look at me like
voice was low, suddenly husky. 'I'm
make you mad again,' he predicted. 'Do you think you can bear it?'

The sudden warmth of his mouth moving hungrily against her lips sent shivers of intense desire through every part of Simone's body. 'I want you!' The words were breathed erotically against her skin as he repeated the demand.

Dear Reader

This month, I would like to ask you to think about the kind of heroine you would like to find in our stories. Do you think she should be sweet and gentle, on the look-out for a man who will be able to care for and nurture her, or should the heroine be able to give as good as she gets, throwing punch for punch, and quite capable of standing up for herself? If you have any opinions on this matter please let us know, so that we can continue to give you the books you want to read!

The Editor

Laura Martin lives in a small Gloucestershire village with her husband, two young children and a lively sheepdog! Laura has a great love of interior design and, together with her husband, has recently completed the renovation of their Victorian cottage. Her hobbies include gardening, the theatre, music and reading, and she finds great pleasure and inspiration from walking daily in the beautiful countryside around her home.

Recent titles by the same author:

GARDEN OF DESIRE

A FOOLISH HEART

BY

LAURA MARTIN

MILLS & BOON LIMITED
ETON HOUSE, 18-24 PARADISE ROAD
RICHMOND, SURREY TW9 1SR

First published in Great Britain 1993
by Mills & Boon Limited

This edition 1993

ISBN 0 263 78182 8

Set in Times Roman 10 on 12 pt.
01-9308-53189 C

Made and printed in Great Britain

CHAPTER ONE

HIS voice was, as usual, low and deeply seductive, each sensually spoken syllable heavy with meaning. She felt his hands, strong and immensely large, around her waist, pulling her towards him. The smouldering gaze told her all she needed to know; Simone registered the gleam of masculine force, saw the blaze of desire reflected in the ebony pools and was aware of her own desire, her own need, matching his. The ache deep down in the pit of her stomach that was so acute, so familiar...

It had been so long...so long...

She looked up into his face and smiled, but something was wrong. He had changed, turned into a stranger with an evil smile. He wouldn't let her go. The vice-like grip held her firmly against the hardened male strength. She felt the taste of his mouth on hers, experienced the shock of his touch as his hands roamed her body.

Where was her baby? Where was she? Simone felt the familiar desperate surge of panic and tried to fight against the inevitable—for this man was leading her now, dragging her away towards the bed...

Simone's vivid blue eyes flashed open. She had called out. The eerie sound still seemed to echo in the room. Her own cry of anguish had woken her. She stared wide-eyed at the ceiling of the pretty peach-coloured bedroom, breathing short shallow breaths, tension gripping her limbs.

It wasn't happening. All past. All gone.

She sat up, aware of the damp heat of her body, and rubbed a shaky hand across her eyes, forcing forgetfulness, trying in vain to obliterate the vivid images of the night.

Why? Simone thought. Why did the nightmare always rear its ugly head when she was beginning to feel good—about herself, about life in general? It was as if her subconscious just couldn't let go, had to keep reminding her, showing Simone Walker that she wasn't as resilient as she liked to believe, that there were still parts of her that could never forget that time, those dreadful subsequent months.

She knew the antidote by now, of course; practice made perfect and she was strong, good at concealing, even from herself, the emotional torment that had never quite gone away.

Simone threw back the bedcovers, shivering a little in the cold of the December morning, and thrust her feet into furry mules. And here she was. Her latest venture. Another place, another beginning. Seven of them altogether, counting this one, since Katy had died.

Simone moved her neck stiffly, rubbed at her sore shoulders and sat slumped on the edge of the bed. It had been a long, bad night. Lethargy hung over her like a heavy cloak. She still felt pretty washed out; the flu had hit her for six, several days ago, and the after-effects were taking time to leave her completely. She knew she had to move and get on, but still she found herself staring into space, reliving the old nightmare over and over again.

In reality it hadn't been anything like that, of course, and in a way that was, she knew, the reason why the nightmare continued to haunt her: she still couldn't forgive herself for allowing him to make love to her; she could never forgive herself for the subsequent events...

Her hands curled into tight fists as she went over everything again in her mind, tears trickling down her cheeks at the memories. Stop it! she commanded of herself in fierce undertones. It's been five years! Life has moved on. Stop torturing yourself like this.

She forced a deep controlling breath and turned to glance at the clock beside the bed, her brow creasing into a despairing frown as she registered the time. Oh, no! It couldn't be as late as that, could it? Almost nine-thirty! She should have been up and dressed hours ago. Simone jumped up and searched frantically for her dressing-gown. After all, today was the big day. Hadn't Mrs White told her a hundred times or more that the lord and master of the house returned from his trip abroad and to make an especially big effort to have everything in order?

Simone racked her befuddled brain and tried to remember the exact time of his arrival. She didn't want to believe it, but for some reason nine-thirty sprang rather easily to mind...

The sound of a car just at that moment increased her fears and, grabbing her towelling dressing-gown from the muddle of bedclothes that indicated she had had a restless night, Simone hurried over to the window.

She peered out at the dull grey morning, half hoping it had been the post van she had heard arriving. But no, there, sweeping majestically into the courtyard, was an altogether more opulent vehicle. A gleaming Rolls-Royce, every inch of its sleek grey chassis polished to within an inch of its extremely short life.

Simone cursed, thrusting her arms into her gown. Mr Travis Steele was here.

The chauffeur got out and walked round with infuriating slowness to open the rear passenger door. Simone, despite everything, watched and waited. She knew she should be frantically getting dressed, because, as Mrs White had informed her, 'Mr Steele's a stickler for punctuality, so you be sure you're ready to greet him on his return, my girl—he especially wants to see you,' but she found herself irresistibly glued to the window.

She was intrigued. This man, her employer of just three weeks, a man she had not as yet seen, struck a curious mixture of fear and awe into the hearts of the staff. Just a mention of his name and their tones altered. Stories of staff dismissed at a moment's notice, of savage reprimands for work that wasn't considered up to scratch had reached her ears. Yet none of his old faithfuls, like Mrs White the housekeeper, or the old gardener, who lived on the edge of the estate, would have a word said against him.

A quick peep, she thought, and then I'll make a dash for it. His appearance was not at all what she had been led to expect. Funny, Simone thought, as she wiped the misted glass and peered awkwardly down at the tall, black-coated figure that emerged from the car below; funny how you built up a picture of someone in your mind out of practically nothing. She had imagined an older, slightly more stocky figure. Mrs White talked a great deal about Mr Steele and she had managed, it seemed from this cursory inspection, to impart quite a lot of misleading information. 'He's large and quite a lot older than you,' she had remembered her saying, and Simone had automatically pictured an overweight man in his forties, when in fact Mrs White, who probably imagined Simone to be little over seventeen herself, clearly meant broad and strikingly tall and definitely much younger—if the easy athletic stride was anything to go by. Simone pressed her nose against the pane of glass. If only the efficient chauffeur hadn't pulled up almost directly outside the front entrance, she couldn't see anything of any substance at all.

She hurriedly left her place at the window as the figure of Travis Steele disappeared into the house, and made a dash for the bathroom. If she cleaned her teeth and washed her face now before dressing, she could return later on and spend more time on her *toilette*, she decided. She might look a little unsophisticated without her blonde hair neatly tied and her usual discreetly applied make-up, but that wouldn't matter—after all, he hadn't seen her before; he wouldn't know the difference.

Simone was in the process of pulling on her bright cerise jumper when there was a sharp rap at the door.

'Hold on a minute!' she mumbled, through the layer of pink wool. 'I'm just getting dressed.'

She thought she heard the click of the door, but dismissed the idea. When she hastily pulled her head through the polo neck of her jumper, she realised with an embarrassed start that she had been right.

'You were informed, I believe, of my wish to see you the minute I arrived. It is precisely...' Travis Steele paused and glanced at the flash of gold at his wrist '...nine-forty, Miss Walker, and you are half dressed!'

Simone swiftly yanked the jumper down to cover her brief lace panties, staring at the tall, rugged figure before her with complete astonishment. 'Do you always barge into ladies' bedrooms without being invited?' Simone snapped impulsively, only remembering, too late, that the man in front of her was undoubtedly her employer, glimpsed just seconds before and, though not necessarily worthy of respect, demanding it nevertheless.

'I will expect you downstairs in five minutes, Miss Walker,' he barked, ignoring her outburst, 'otherwise consider your contract terminated!'

Simone gazed, open-mouthed, and watched as he turned without so much as an introduction and departed from her bedroom.

Even when the door had been snapped shut she still found herself staring at the place where the large, imposing figure had stood. Of all the arrogant swines! she thought, half shaking her head in disbelief at this astonishing first meeting with her employer. Did he always behave like that?

The many rumours that had reached her ears since she had begun working in the house seeped into her mind again. 'He won't stand any nonsense, you know!' That had been one of Mrs White's favourite phrases, she remembered now, that and, 'Oh, he's a one for the ladies, that he is!'

Perhaps that was why he barged into my room, Simone thought bitterly, just on the off-chance of catching me in my underwear!

She glanced down now and tried to work out if he had seen more than he should have. Thank goodness she hadn't yet drawn the curtains! Like everything else in this impressive house, they were of the best quality, beautifully made with thick linings. She gave an inward sigh of relief, and went over to draw them back, allowing the feeble December light into the room. It stood to reason that he couldn't have seen a great deal of her, just as she'd seen precious little of him. The outline, of course, and that had been terrifying enough, Simone admitted honestly, but not a great deal more.

She wasn't a fool. She couldn't afford to be. Simone made sure she appeared downstairs before the five minutes had run its course. She had not a shadow of a doubt that Travis Steele would fire her on the spot if she didn't follow his orders and, much as she would have loved to defy her self-important boss and tell him what he could do with his job, she knew she couldn't even contemplate such drastic, impulsive action. This post was her lifeline—money had seemed to slip straight through her fingers recently, and to walk out now without thinking about where she would go, what she would do next, would be extremely foolish—besides which, of course, there was Jake to consider.

Mrs White's expression showed extreme disapproval when Simone asked where to find Mr Steele. 'He's in the library,' she said with a slight shake of her head, 'and I'll tell you now, young lady, he's not best pleased.'

'I've worked that one out for myself,' Simone replied, ignoring the 'I told you so' expression. 'Do you know he practically barged into my bedroom just now?'

'Ah, well, he dislikes certain things,' Mrs White muttered darkly, 'and late rising is one of them. You do know the time, I presume? It's not far off ten o'clock! Didn't I warn you to be on your toes this morning?'

Simone decided against giving her perfectly reasonable explanations to the housekeeper. It would be a waste of breath, she could see that, and after all it was Mr Steele she had to convince—no one else. Once she'd explained about being ill, once she'd smiled and used the charm that was part and parcel of Simone Walker, he wouldn't think so badly of her.

She forced herself to knock confidently on the library door, despite the butterflies that insisted on fluttering around inside her stomach and which increased tenfold with every second he made her wait, so that in the end, after another, less confident knock and more seconds, she gently opened the door and stuck her head around.

'Did I say enter?' a crisp voice enquired, from behind the back of the huge black leather chair that was placed in front of an equally huge leather-topped desk.

Simone hovered, in two minds whether to go back out or stay where she was. 'I... I thought the room was empty,' she murmured nervously.

'In which case, why enter?'

The swivel chair moved around inch by inch and as if in slow motion, and Simone saw her ill-tempered employer properly for the first time. Her movement stilled. She felt the surge of shock and panic slice through her as she catalogued the broad figure, noted the black hair swept back from an intelligent brow, the sharp black suit, the black polo shirt, worn beneath, that gave a clue to style and taste and possible unconventionality.

She would never forget the moment, not as long as she lived, she thought.

A sharp panther-like image, stark and positive, and menacing, sitting only a few feet from her. Every inch of the angular face visible to her. Every inch remembered with such heart-stopping clarity.

'You're staring, Miss Walker. Is there something you'd like to say?'

She stared some more, and then, realising belatedly that he must have spoken, shifted her gaze and said croakily, 'P-pardon?'

His eyes, dark and impossibly familiar, stared back at her, assessing her face, her figure, her whole astonished self for several seconds. 'I asked if there was something you wish to say. Is there a problem, Miss Walker?' His seductive mouth curled attractively. 'You're beginning to look as if you're half-witted, when I know for a fact that you are more than mentally able. Miss Walker!'

The insistent ring of her name had the desired effect, snapping Simone out of her supposed mental lethargy. 'I'm sorry,' she mumbled, straightening up, forcing the present to push away the past, 'I was thinking. I...' Simone gulped and took a breath. 'What was it you were saying?'

'You look pale, Miss Walker. Are you sure you've fully recovered from your illness?' He held her with ebony eyes, assessing Simone's delicate wan face for two, maybe three slow seconds. 'You've had a bout of flu, I believe?'

'Yes, that's right,' Simone replied.

'Hardly the best way to start your new post.'

'I couldn't help catching the flu!' Simone retorted defensively.

'Did I say you could?' Travis Steele replied smoothly. 'I merely meant that it must have been rather inconvenient for everyone—yourself included. Jake, I trust, was kept well away during the indisposition?'

'Of course!' Simone answered, struggling now to keep even a modicum of civility in her tone. 'I sent him work on the days when I felt very ill and Mrs White kept an eye on him for me.'

She hung her head, unable to continue looking into his face. The sight of him, here, only a few feet from her, was too much to take in. He didn't recognise her—not that she had ever expected him to—and that was something at least.

A one for the ladies! Ah, yes! He had been that, indeed. Simone licked her drying lips and tried not to remember that night five years ago. She was hoping for the impossible. Scarcely a day went by without some mental reference to that time. She had been swept along on a sea of passion by this man and, no matter which way she looked at it, she still couldn't forgive herself, forgive him, for altering her life so drastically, and she hadn't even known his name till now...

A vivid image of the two of them flashed unbidden into her mind. It was all she could see, all she could feel... She felt weak at the memory.

'You have been here a little over three weeks, Miss Walker—how has Jake responded?'

He was saying something; she would have to attend. Simone dragged herself together, found composure from somewhere, listened, forced herself to speak. 'I'm sorry...' She shook her head slightly, indicating she hadn't heard or didn't understand, or both.

Travis Steele released a taut breath. Clearly he was having difficulty keeping patience. 'What do you feel you have achieved so far with Jake?' he asked, slowing his question to half speed to make sure it was clearly understood.

'Achieved?' Simone frowned and half shook her head. Her brain felt like suet. God! What could she say? What did he mean? 'I...I feel I've made some progress,' she murmured, after a hefty pause. 'Jake is—er—beginning to respond to me now.' She paused, gave a little shrug, trembling beneath the hard, efficient gaze.

'You were selected, I believe, from a number of highly qualified candidates,' Travis Steele remarked cuttingly. 'Is this the best response you can come up with? I had hoped for a more professional assessment.'

Simone pursed her lips angrily at his scathing tones. Just standing here before him took all her strength. It took every ounce of mental power not to cry aloud that she hated the very sight of him, to tell him crisply what he could do with his damned teaching post, never mind coming up with Jake's progress report!

The door burst open just then, forestalling the angry reply that was on Simone's lips, and Jake ran into the room. He sped like a tornado across the room and practically threw himself on to Travis Steele's lap. Simone watched, confident of his reaction, sure inside of the cool, perfunctory greeting Travis Steele would give to the child. Such a controlled, arrogant man. A bachelor, who would have no idea how to treat a recently bereaved child. Poor Jake having him for a guardian! Poor, poor child!

He lifted Jake into his arms and held him close, enclosing the slight, fragile body in huge, powerful arms, swivelling around in the chair, so that Jake gave an unusual shout of delight and asked for more when they stopped.

'No more, Jake, not now anyway. I have to speak to Miss Walker,' he explained firmly after a moment, unworried, it seemed, that this display of emotional normality should be witnessed by her. 'Give me five minutes and then I'll come and see you,' he added, placing Jake gently back on to his feet. 'We'll do anything you like then, OK?'

'Miss Walker promised me we could go for a walk in the woods this morning,' Jake replied, with a heart-warming degree of excitement. 'We're going to search out all sorts of things. Will you come with us? I've got a case with a special magnifying glass to find tracks and a notebook to write things down and everything, haven't I, Miss Walker?' He turned towards Simone and gave her a brilliant smile which partly succeeded in dispelling the misery that was steadily swamping her.

Simone nodded and wished she could enjoy the moment more. This change in the child was quite remarkable; he looked happier than she had ever seen him. 'Yes, Jake, you have.'

'So will you come?' Jake asked again, turning anxious, hopeful eyes to the man who was unfortunately—as far as Simone was concerned anyway—his guardian.

'Of course,' Travis replied, without the slightest hesitation. 'Now run along and get ready. Miss Walker and I will be with you shortly.

'Well, things aren't quite as bad as I had imagined,' he drawled, a slight smile hovering at the edges of his mouth. 'Jake seems to have taken to you; that's something in your favour at least.' He eyed Simone with aggravating superiority. 'He doesn't find it easy to accept new people—but then you were told that in the beginning.'

'I was given a brief outline, yes,' Simone replied coolly. 'Not enough information, though, in my opinion, to help the child——'

'You were given the information I wished you to have. No more, no less,' he informed her cuttingly. 'May I remind you, Miss Walker, that you are here to supervise Jake's academic progress? There are others who will take care of his emotional well-being.'

Like you? Simone queried silently. You haven't got an ounce of emotion in your body! Poor Jake!

He rose then and walked towards the door, making it clear as he opened it that the interrogation, reprimand, call it what you would, was at an end. 'This has not been a particularly impressive beginning, Miss Walker, has it?' he remarked curtly, blocking the doorway with his huge frame, so that escape was agonisingly postponed.

Simone glanced up into the all-too-handsome features and felt a shiver of awareness traverse her whole body. Oh, why did he have to look so incredible? Every inch the successful businessman, every inch a man of the world. His lashes were still wonderfully thick, she noted, shrouding eyes that were still as black as the night...

She was staring and Travis Steele could see that she was. Simone noted the gleam of interest in his expression and hastily lowered her eyes in confusion. 'N-no, I suppose not.'

'I expect more from my employees, Miss Walker,' he informed her with characteristic bluntness. 'Far more. Don't make me regret having hired you.'

The rest of the day passed by in a blur.

Simone held on somehow, playing the part of teacher, doing her best to ignore Travis Steele, concentrating wholly on Jake, bombarding him with ideas and questions and games, forcing every ounce of composure to rise to the surface so that by the time evening fell she was absolutely exhausted, both mentally and physically.

Simone wearily stapled the last piece of coloured paper to the wall and then stood back, hands on hips, to admire the effect. She'd had enough. Her brain ached with continually refusing to think, her heart ached because seeing him brought back memories . . . of that night . . . of Katy. Tears pricked at her eyes and she hastily brought up a hand to brush them away.

The picture looked good, she thought with determined effort, bright and cheerful. The Christmas scene was beginning to take shape. Jake would be pleased to see his efforts on display when he came in next morning.

Simone ran her fingers through her long, silky blonde hair and rubbed at the ache in the small of her back. Perversity had kept her here in the schoolroom long after hours. Jake had been excused lessons to be with Travis and Simone had been curtly informed by him that the rest of the day was hers to spend as she wished.

She stooped down and began picking up the scraps of paper that were scattered around the floor. He had expected her to lounge around, of course, drive off in her bright yellow Mini to town to make the most of her free hours. Instead she had stayed, shutting herself in the schoolroom, working hard, thinking even harder about what she should do, how she could possibly cope.

She wished she had gone away now. She wished she had had the sense to get in her car and put her foot down and just drive.

'I'm impressed—do you always work this late?'

The voice, so unexpected and out of place in the quietness of the room, deep and undoubtedly belonging to only one man, startled Simone so much that she jumped, clutching a hand instinctively to her heart. She closed her eyes for a fraction of a second, took a huge steadying breath and then raised herself up from the floor and looked over to where the voice had come from.

Travis Steele was leaning nonchalantly against a bright poster, an apparition appearing out of nowhere, dark and dynamic, full of animal magnetism, watching her.

Simone licked nervously at her lips and swallowed, aware of the sudden flush that had leapt to her cheeks, the racing beat of her heart. 'Y-you startled me,' she murmured jerkily.

'Evidently,' he replied, with a smoothness that made Simone feel in no way better. 'My apologies.' He moved from the position that he had assumed goodness knew how long ago, and moved towards Simone, to where she had been working, glancing up at the huge wall, which was partly covered with painstakingly made figures, representing scenes from the Nativity. 'Looks good,' he drawled, 'but isn't it a bit early? We're only just in December.'

'I realise that,' Simone replied steadily, glancing up at Jake's work with steadfast eyes, refusing to let his easy criticism annoy her. 'But all this takes time. Jake and I should just about have it finished by Christmas week.' She moved away, nervous hands thrust into the pockets of her rich green pinafore, twisting the handkerchief that was inside around and around her clenched fingers. 'Believe it or not, but I like things to be done properly,' she explained stiffly. 'No rushing, no messy work. By the time Christmas arrives I want Jake to be extremely proud of his efforts.'

'And so he should be—I never realised he had such artistic talents. You're obviously bringing out the best in him.' He scanned the wall some more and then turned and wandered about the room, inspecting. 'It's late,' he murmured after a while, glancing casually at the distinctive and unmistakably expensive watch at his wrist. 'Do you often work in here at this hour?' White teeth flashed irresistibly against his smooth, tanned skin. 'Or am I being treated to a show of dedication to make up for the bad start you made this morning?'

She glared at him, ignoring the degree of lightness that had been in his tone, and found that her voice held a satisfying amount of ice. 'I do my job well, Mr Steele,' she told him, frost clinging to every syllable, 'whatever you might think! I spend most evenings in here, going over work, getting ready for the next day. I...' Her voice trailed away as she looked across and registered his vaguely amused expression. She took a determined breath. 'Was there something you particularly wanted, Mr Steele?' she added. 'Only, as you so rightly pointed out, it's late and I am rather busy.'

'I want to talk to you about Jake,' he informed her. 'Your vague sentence this morning about his progress was hardly adequate. I would like to discuss details of his development.'

Simone bent down and began scooping up armfuls of coloured paper from the floor. 'He's getting along fine,' she replied edgily. 'I'm very pleased with him.'

Ebony eyes narrowed. 'You're telling me there are no problems?'

Simone hesitated, and thought about any number of bad days when she felt like tearing her hair out because of Jake's sullen, disruptive attitude. 'It's early days,' she murmured neutrally, evading the disbelieving dark eyes. 'He's still settling down.'

'I can take the truth, Miss Walker,' he replied drily. 'If I'm to help Jake, I need an honest reply.'

'That was an honest reply!' Simone flashed. 'I'm not in the habit of lying about any of my pupils.'

'So his behaviour has been exemplary, has it?' he demanded with sudden fierceness. 'I have no need to worry at all that Mrs White has mentioned incidents, one of which involved dropping a chair from a second-floor window which narrowly missed the gardener, another where blue paint was thrown all round this room!'

Simone took a breath and managed somehow to meet the blazing eyes. 'She told you that?'

'Under duress. Mrs White was loath to impart the information, but she could see in the end it would be for the best. I am Jake's guardian, after all. Did he pour the paint deliberately?' he persisted. 'I hear you got your fair share of it.' His eyes probed hers unmercifully. 'Was that the case?'

'No. Oh, no, I'm sure it was an accident,' Simone replied swiftly, picturing the mess that the bright blue paint had caused. 'He was swinging around and somehow the pot lid flew off. We washed the room and my dress and——'

'Covering up when Jake behaves abominably isn't going to help either of us, Miss Walker,' he cut in crisply. 'I need to be kept in the picture if I'm to help him.'

Simone stuffed the waste paper she held into the black bin-liner and turned to face him with pursed lips. 'I like to be fair,' she replied insistently. 'You shouldn't have asked Mrs White; she wasn't here when it happened. You should have come to me first.'

'I'm here now and you still haven't answered my question, Miss Walker!' he replied impatiently. 'I wish to know exactly how Jake has behaved while I've been away. Were those episodes isolated affairs or not?'

Simone glanced nervously into the taut, angular face for a second, found patience and yet more control from somewhere. 'Well, all right, then,' she conceded flatly, 'Jake has been a little...' the word 'obnoxious' sprang to her mind, but that wouldn't have sounded so good, so she substituted '... difficult. But I'm sure,' she added swiftly, 'that, given time, you'll see great improvement.'

'Let's hope so.' His voice held a grim note and something more besides—weariness perhaps? Despondency?

She watched as he lounged casually on one of the desks, dwarfing the furniture, dominating the space around him. Like an alien being, Simone thought fleetingly, eyeing the broad, rugged frame, dressed all in black, in this child-size room, designed especially for Jake.

'So where is Jake now?' she asked croakily, moving cautiously around him, tidying with an intensity that covered her unease, because he was still here, alone in this room with her, intimidating her with his poised masculine presence, causing treacherous thoughts to leap into her mind.

Travis ran a large hand through springy black hair. 'Having supper in the kitchen. Here, you missed this.' He bent down and casually retrieved a handful of scrap paper from beneath a desk, strolling over, adding the bundle to the bin-liner Simone held.

For the briefest of moments, his long, tanned fingers came into contact with Simone's hand, a breath of a touch, but enough. Enough to make Simone snatch back, removing her pale fingers from contact with his as if she'd been stung.

'What is it?' His dark eyes narrowed with brief concern. 'Did you cut yourself on something?'

Simone shook her head, her mouth slightly open as she struggled to come up with some sort of explanation for her pronounced, almost violent reaction. 'Er—no, no, just a scrape,' she mumbled hastily. 'The edges of paper can be quite sharp, can't they?' She thrust her perfectly unscathed hands back into her pinafore pockets and escaped his probing stare by moving to her desk to retrieve some books. 'I'm afraid I have to go now,' she informed him with as much cool as she could muster. She glanced out through the classroom windows at the pitch blackness of the winter evening and wished there was somewhere she could *go* to. 'If you wish to discuss Jake's progress more fully, perhaps we could talk tomorrow. The swimming instructor arrives for his lesson at nine. We could talk at length then.'

'I rather thought we'd talk tonight, Miss Walker. Tomorrow is difficult for me. I have an important business meeting, which will take up most of the day.' He spoke in clipped tones—clearly the lord and master did not like being organised. 'Have you eaten?'

Simone hesitated, casting Travis a wary glance. 'Not yet. Mrs White kindly said she would prepare me a tray in my room for later.'

'I see. Well, we'll talk tonight, then—over dinner. I'll go and inform Mrs White of the altered arrangements.'

'No!' Simone found her voice just as he opened the door.

Travis Steele turned, raising a brow in surprise at her strident tone, regarding Simone with interest as if her refusal was a new experience for him.

Which it probably was, Simone thought, as she nervously moved piles of paper around on her desk, her eyes unseeing, in an attempt to cover her awkwardness.

Most women, given the opportunity, would undoubtedly jump at the chance of an invitation to dinner with a man like Travis Steele. A millionaire at thirty, that was what Mrs White had murmured in reverent tones, probably one of the most eligible bachelors in the country, surely one of the most handsome. Oh, yes, most women. But not Simone Walker. She half shook her head, as if the reality of him looming tall and faintly menacing in the room could be altered somehow, just by desperate wishing.

'I'm very tired,' Simone added. 'I've been unwell...'

'In that case,' he informed her in tones that brooked no argument, 'I will do my best to make our conversation as untaxing as possible. Eight o'clock, Miss Walker.' He ran raking eyes over her rather dishevelled figure, taking in her crumpled pinafore and uncombed hair with a glance that left Simone feeling stripped. 'I suggest you dress for dinner,' he instructed pointedly. 'It will make you feel better.' And with that final command he left the room.

CHAPTER TWO

SIMONE glanced across at the carriage clock beside the bed. Its Roman numerals glowed in the half-light; it was exactly seven forty-five.

She sighed and turned back to the window, gazing up at the stars. Two hours of thinking, of remembering, of trying to work out what to do. It was a nightmare. Only this time if she pinched herself she didn't wake up—this was real. This was happening. And she still couldn't quite believe it.

He didn't recognise her—that was something, she supposed. Five years was a long time and of course she had been someone else then—a stranger, even to herself...

Simone could remember every minute of that whole day. By taking the wrong path she had altered the course of her life to an immeasurable degree.

Why had she allowed Colin's hateful words to get to her? He had been an immature idiot, not worth a moment of her time.

But of course she could say that now, look back with the benefit of hindsight. In those days people's opinion had mattered.

It had shocked her that Colin had expected sex on the first date—not that she let him know that, of course. She had refused, quite reasonably, she had thought, had continued to spurn his advances. By the fifth date, Colin, who considered himself quite a catch at the college, had declared to just about the whole canteen that quiet Simone Walker had a problem—she was 'sexless', as 'cold as the ice-box in a refrigerator'—those had been two of his more polite phrases, she remembered.

Something inside Simone had shrivelled and died that lunchtime. Perhaps if she'd been more outgoing, more worldly-wise, she would have seen Colin for what he was, but she wasn't. She was insecure and painfully shy, with few friends, and every word hurt her like hell.

So fate had taken a hand. And when Jenny, the leader of the rather wild group of girls, had suggested a night out, called Colin a creep and told her to forget him, she felt tons better.

She could see it had just been a hilarious challenge to them—transforming dowdy Simone Walker, with her medium-coloured hair and her medium-sized figure, into someone who looked as if she had just stepped out from the pages of a fashion shoot, but, for her, the transformation had lifted her out from the depths of depression, giving her a chance, the ammunition to prove a very important point.

With dyed black hair, borrowed clothes and even the unlikely, exotic name of Chantelle for the evening, Simone had stepped determinedly into a rather exclusive nightclub and become someone else.

Travis Steele had entered late, she remembered. And he had taken her breath away. 'Mean and moody' described him exactly. Dressed in a crisp, sharp suit, standing head and shoulders above most of the crowd, he had blown away all other men in the room.

He had a presence, an indefinable quality, that even now, all these years later, Simone couldn't pin down. She had been unable to take her eyes off him. She just couldn't help it; neither, it seemed, could most of the female population in the room. He had had many offers; several confident glamour types approached, attempted to strike up conversation, all to no avail. He had sat at the bar, drink in hand, surveying the pulsating mass with an indifferent, superior eye.

And then his dark, impenetrable gaze had found Simone's. But instead of skimming away and moving on to someone else, as she had expected it to do, it had lingered and lingered and then a slow, seductive smile had transformed the superior expression and Simone had found herself rising and strolling confidently over, inventing a slow, sensual walk, even a slightly huskier voice, because of course it was all a game—a man as incredible as this couldn't possibly want *her*.

But he had.

It was as if he had mesmerised her somehow. She had scarcely been able to believe she was doing this, talking to him, smiling confidently at him. Certainly Jenny and the gang had watched agog as she perched on a stool and accepted his offer of a drink.

'So why don't we go somewhere that's a little quieter?' he had drawled, after Simone had consumed a couple of the nightclub's potent cocktails and he had held her in his arms and moved her around the dance-floor with slow sensuality. 'You can tell me your life story.'

Except that there had been precious little conversation.

Travis Steele had begun to remove her clothing the moment they had stepped into his swish chrome and white apartment.

It had been incredible. Looking back all these years later, she could still feel the urgency that he had generated within her. Frigid Simone Walker had been lost the moment his mouth had trailed across her skin, the moment his hands had roamed beneath her borrowed jacket.

He had been sure and he had been smooth and he had seduced her without any effort at all.

The sheets had felt wonderfully cool against her heated body as he had lain her gently back on to the bed. Simone could remember that her one and only moment of doubt had been then, that point of release, while he undressed before her. For just a second she had tensed as the momentous implications of such a course crowded in on her, pushing aside the heady mixture of her new-found sexuality and desire for this man.

But then, almost as if he had sensed her indecision, Travis had bent and murmured gentle words, spoken to her as if he really *cared*, kissed her with such wonderful erotic intenseness that any fleeting doubts had been blown away and she had melted in his arms and trusted herself to him completely.

'You're a virgin!' The words had been breathed with incredulity in the dim glow of his bedroom.

Simone had closed her eyes and clung to him, glad that the searing pain had ended, feeling the salty tears of unexplained emotion trickling down her cheeks.

He must have felt them, for, instead of rolling away from her as she had expected, he had brushed back the strange black strands of hair from her face and kissed each moist cheek, each eyelid with infinite care. 'I hurt you. I'm so sorry,' he had whispered huskily.

She hadn't been able to speak. What was there to say? So many emotions had been bombarding her, so many thoughts. She had allowed a perfect stranger to make love to her...

She had known she should leave. But he had taken her in his arms then and held her close and succeeded with such ease in keeping her there that Simone cringed now to think about it.

Miraculously she had slept for a while, waking in the middle of the night to find Travis beside her, propped up on one elbow watching her.

'You're beautiful.'

She knew that she wasn't. But his voice had been deep and husky and it had mesmerised her so much that she would have believed virtually anything. Each syllable had dripped sensuality.

Looking back, Simone wondered how she could have been so naïve. Two words, a kiss. How could she have fallen for it all?

He had held her gaze for a long moment, just to make sure that she was convinced of his sincerity, and then his mouth had descended with possessive hunger and he had slowly and deliberately shown Simone how incredible sex could be.

When she had awoken next morning he was gone.

Deep down, Simone had known that the apartment was empty, but still she had gone from room to room looking for him, looking for some sign that would save her from thinking the worst.

Nothing. No note, no flower left romantically on the pillow, no message scrawled with a decisive hand telling her to wait for his return.

This was not the movies. This was real life. She had been used and discarded and she had to leave, before the humiliation got any worse.

Searching out her clothes had been a nightmare. She had scrabbled around furiously, half dreading, half hoping that he might walk in any minute, sick with anticipation. Her scarf had defeated her, but apart from that one small item there was no sign, as she left, that she had ever been there...

Simone felt the touch of a tiny hand and she jumped, looking down through glistening eyes, to where Jake, adorably vulnerable, dressed in striped pyjamas and clutching a moth-eaten teddy, looked up at her with large brown eyes.

She took a huge steadying breath, smiled and then scooped him up on to her lap, suddenly glad of his solid warmth.

'Look at the stars, Jake,' she whispered, hugging him close. 'Aren't they beautiful?'

He was sleepy, thumb plunged comfortingly into his mouth. Simone stroked back his hair and they sat together in the moonlit room in silence.

Katy would have been almost five now...Jake's cousin... Simone closed her eyes and tightened her grip so that Jake wriggled a little on her lap. She mustn't think about that now...not now.

'What's he doing here?' Travis's voice sliced unmercifully through her thoughts. Simone jerked her head to the doorway and felt a shudder of apprehension as her eyes surveyed his rugged frame, silhouetted almost menacingly by the moonlight.

He moved towards the window-seat and stared down at Jake. The angled planes of his face were half hidden in shadow, but Simone knew instinctively that he was ill-pleased. 'He should be in bed.'

It was an effort to talk. Simone's throat had dried and constricted at the sudden sound of his voice at the still breathtaking sight of him. 'He... he just came in to say goodnight,' she managed croakily, glancing down at Jake, who was now fast asleep, blissfully unaware of his uncle's anger, curled up into a ball like a small, plump puppy.

'Does he do this often?'

'Sometimes.' Simone gazed back at the stars. She couldn't look at his face in the half-darkness; it reminded her of that night, so long ago. She swallowed painfully. 'Does it matter?'

'Of course it matters!' He crouched down beside Jake and stared for a long while at the reposing figure. 'I don't approve. You're his teacher, not his nursemaid! Here, give him to me. I'll take him back to his bed.'

'No!' Simone held him tightly, her arms curling protectively around his warm body. 'I'll carry him.' She tried to raise herself up from the window-seat, but Jake was awkwardly placed and she knew it was impossible the minute she tried to move.

'Here, let me.' Travis Steele reached forward and Simone steeled herself, stiffening every sinew as she felt the touch of his hands, the shocking brush of his skin against her own.

'You are not, presumably, planning to dine in that?' He sauntered back into the room, after depositing Jake back into his bedroom, lounged against the wall, his voice amused and slightly scornful.

It was gone eight and he was dressed for dinner. Simone, much to her own annoyance, had immediately noticed the Armani suit, smelt the clean freshness of his distinctive cologne. She glanced down at the thick fleecy dressing-gown she was wearing and realised the contrast between them was laughable. Except, of course, she wasn't in the mood for hilarity.

'I'm not coming down at all!' Simone retorted icily. She rose from the window, wrapping her arms protectively around her body. 'I'm very tired and I need some sleep.'

'You also, presumably, need this job?' He moved towards her with slow deliberation. 'No more excuses, please, Miss Walker! I'm beginning to feel as if I have the plague at the very least.' He was close, studying her delicate features with an amused, derisive expression. 'What is it? I don't suppose you would care to tell me?'

Simone struggled to stand her ground, her eyes darting for possible means of escape. She licked nervously at dry, dry lips. He had lost none of his presence, none of his incredible male vitality. 'I... I don't know what you mean!' Her voice was shamefully faint, totally unconvincing.

'Oh, I think you do,' he drawled, thrusting hands casually into his pockets. 'You see, for some unfathomable reason I only have to come within striking distance and you jump a mile. For instance, if I move a little closer, like this, so that we are almost touching... You see?' Ebony brows raised as Simone stepped back a pace. 'Quite remarkable.'

'Mr Steele...' Simone forced as much icy emphasis as she could muster. 'Mr Steele, will you please leave my bedroom?'

'I want you to dine with me tonight.' Another pace forward, another step back, Simone's last, because now she had come up against the wall. 'Agree,' he murmured in warning tones. 'Do as I ask, Miss Walker. I am not used to being disobeyed.'

His eyes were mesmerising her. Simone gulped and found that there didn't seem to be enough oxygen, enough space. Treacherous pictures of long ago flashed into her mind—his broad muscular body entwined with hers, the look of hungry desire that had melted her resistance so effectively... She felt so angry suddenly, so used and cheated. How could he stand here like this, playing such damned arrogant games?

Simone raised her hand; the need to strike that superior expression clean from his face was suddenly totally overwhelming. She didn't give a damn about the consequences, she just knew it was the right thing to do.

He was miles too quick for her. His fingers coiled around her raised wrist like several small snakes crushing prey. 'Interesting,' he drawled. 'A temper! I had no idea.'

'Let me go!' she spat. 'Don't you dare touch me!'

'Do you often resort to physical abuse, Miss Walker? Become so irrationally uptight?'

Simone's free hand clenched fiercely together at her side. Irrationally uptight? She was frantic. Five years ago, she had allowed this arrogant man to do with her as he willed. She had suffered for months—no, years—afterwards.

That unforgettable day when she had found that she carried his child had been horrendous. Blind panic had consumed her for weeks and then when her pregnancy had been too difficult to bear alone, too obvious, the arguments, the endless silence, because she refused to tell her parents who the father was. Hell! She hadn't known herself! Names and professional profiles hadn't come into it. And even if she had known everything that there was to know about this man there would have been nothing on this earth that would have persuaded her to go back, find him, tell him . . . Life was cruel; seeing him again like this only reaffirmed that fact.

'You can't force me to dine with you,' she managed tightly.

'No?' His lips curved into a predatory smile. 'Well, let's just put it this way, shall we? If you're not down-stairs ready to eat by——' he glanced at his watch, the luminous dial reflecting clearly in the moonlit room '—nine o'clock, I will deduce that you're not sufficiently interested in Jake's well-being, and therefore not suitable for the post of governess.'

'You'd sack me, just like that?' Her voice quivered with hating disbelief.

'I have high standards, Miss Walker. If you do not come up to them, then that is your problem, not mine.'

Simone released and inhaled a much needed breath of oxygen. 'I'll...I'll be ready in ten minutes,' she breathed, staring stonily into his face.

He released her wrist, a furiously annoying expression of satisfaction on his face. 'Make it five,' he commanded softly, 'and I'll forgive you for your attempted act of violence.'

She dressed in a daze, once he had exited her bedroom, locking the door behind him, grabbing the first vaguely appropriate item from the wardrobe—black velvet ski-pants and a long, loose-fitting tunic top in the same rich fabric. She would have put on a sack, had there been one available, but this outfit satisfied some of her requirements at least: the fabric was thick, the cut disguised much of her womanly shape and covered almost all of her flesh. It was too elegant, unfortunately, and it made her look more attractive than she wanted, but it was all she had.

Simone sat at her dressing-table and regarded her reflection intently. She would resign tonight. There was little else she could do. To stay here a moment longer than was necessary would be the height of self-torture and foolishness. She applied her make-up with shaking hands, caught her long blonde hair into a silky bow at the nape of her neck. She would go right away, hide somewhere until Christmas was well and truly over. But where to go? And more importantly, what to live on? Practical thoughts spilled urgently, spoiling her resolutions.

She stood up and half shook her head. No matter; resign first, think later.

'Miss Walker!' Jake's small voice reached her ears just as she was passing by his door.

Simone hesitated and then went in. 'What is it, Jake?' He was cuddled under his duvet, just his small round face visible in the red glow of his night light.

'Can we go on another nature trail tomorrow?'

Simone knelt down and stroked the thatch of blond hair. 'I'm not sure,' she murmured. 'We'll have to see what your uncle has planned.'

'He can't be with me tomorrow,' Jake informed her regretfully; 'he's got to go somewhere.'

Simone hid her look of annoyance. He had been away for three weeks and now he was off somewhere else! She smiled, tousled Jake's hair and nodded. 'OK, then, we can.' She stood up. 'Now close your eyes and go to sleep,' she instructed firmly. 'It's getting very late.'

'Miss Walker!'

'Yes, Jake.'

'I like having you here.'

Simone hesitated at the door and closed her eyes for a second, fighting back the tightness in her throat. 'I'm pleased, Jake. Thank you.' What to do? Simone leant against the bedroom door and closed her eyes in desperation. Think first perhaps, resign later? Or resign now as she had planned and pretend that Jake's life wouldn't be affected, that she wouldn't hurt him?

When Simone finally moved self-consciously into the impressively ornate drawing-room, her mind was in utter turmoil, the same questions repeating themselves over and over. What to do? Stay or resign? Think of her own sanity or the continued well-being of Jake? He needed her. She knew it without doubt. In the three weeks since she arrived the change in him had been quite noticeable.

'You seem intent on perpetuating my disapproval, Miss Walker!' Travis Steele glanced pointedly down at his watch, his deep tones slicing through her indecision. 'It is now eight-thirty.'

Simone released a shaky breath. 'Jake woke up.'

'In that case you should have sent for Mrs White; she would have seen to him.'

'But he wanted me!'

Travis moved to the corner of the room where any number of bottles resided on a tray and began pouring. 'Perhaps I haven't made myself clear enough,' he replied evenly. 'You are Jake's teacher, no more than that. You were employed to take over his educational welfare, until such time as he is deemed ready to attend school.' He handed her a tall glass and took a draught of the amber liquid in his own. 'Emotional involvement is not required. Is that clear?'

Simone took a sip of her wine. It was cold and dry and refreshing, but it did nothing to quell the anger that was rising through every part of her. 'I'm sorry, Mr Steele,' she said crisply, 'but unlike some people I am unable to switch my emotions on and off like a tap. Jake and I have formed a bond. We like each other.' She tilted her chin determinedly and threw him a scornful glance. 'Perhaps you find such simple honest feelings hard to comprehend but——'

'Meaning?'

His voice was dangerously low. Simone recognised the warning signs and forced herself to back off. She shook her head, managed somehow to meet the probing signs. 'I can't change the way I am,' she murmured. 'I teach the only way I know how. The fact that Jake has progressed since I've arrived surely proves my methods work.'

'And when you leave—what then?' Travis demanded savagely. 'Allowing Jake to become attached, allowing pity and sympathy to get in the way of your professional aims——'

'How can you be so hard?' Simone breathed. 'The poor child's lost everything!'

'I am well aware of Jake's circumstances!' Travis grated. 'His mother was my younger sister, his father my business partner. When their bodies were hurled off the motorway and cut from the wreckage, it was I who had to identify them.'

His words stung her into silence. Simone glanced down at her hands. 'I'm sorry,' she murmured inadequately.

'For what?' he demanded. 'For their death? Save your sympathy, Miss Walker. It was an accident. It's over. Life has moved on!' He opened the double oak doors that led through to the dining-room. 'Now let's eat. And over dinner you will tell me about Jake's academic progress.'

The food was delicious, but Simone struggled to consume more than a few mouthfuls. She pushed the succulent steak absent-mindedly around on her plate for a while and then sat back.

'Not hungry?'

Simone raised her face and saw that ebony eyes were surveying her carefully. 'Not particularly, no.'

'I went over your c.v. earlier today,' Travis informed her, raising his glass of wine to his lips. 'You have a fine list of qualifications.'

Simone allowed herself a nod. 'Yes.'

'Clearly you have worked extremely hard.'

'Implying, of course, that I must have struggled!' Simone flashed back. 'Too difficult to believe that I have a fine brain, that I gained my degree on simple intelligence!'

'Did I say that?' he enquired softly.

'You didn't need to,' Simone replied tightly; 'it was written all over your face!'

'You took this job in the first instance, I believe, because it was a short-term contract,' Travis continued, almost as if Simone hadn't spoken. 'That's correct, isn't it?'

Simone moved uneasily in her seat. 'Yes.'

'You seem to like moving about a lot; seven posts over the last five years, I believe?'

'That's right,' Simone agreed, almost defiantly. 'I get bored easily. But this was discussed at my interview. Your personal assistant listened to my reasons and accepted them.'

'No family, no ties?'

'None. My parents are both dead. Look,' Simone added hurriedly, 'I thought we were going to talk about Jake.'

'We are. First, though, I'd like to find out a little about you. As you know I was unable at the last moment to attend the interviews——'

'And I'm being interviewed now—is that it?'

Travis lounged back in his chair and gave a sardonic twist of his mouth. 'Let's just say I'm going over a few points. I have every faith in Kara, my assistant, but I would just like to satisfy myself with a few additional questions.'

Simone blanched at his words, her heart thudding loudly and forcibly beneath the black velvet. She swallowed nervously, picking up her napkin, twisting it tightly between her fingers. 'I won't be interrogated, Mr Steele,' she informed him shakily. 'My private life is something I wish to keep just that—private!'

He threw her a quizzical, almost disbelieving look. 'Interrogation?'

'That's what it feels like!' Simone retorted, blushing furiously beneath his puzzled gaze.

'I intended us to have a relaxed conversation,' he informed her sharply, 'I don't believe I mentioned interrogation of your private life!'

'No?'

'No! Of course,' Travis added infuriatingly, 'now you have succeeded in arousing my interest. In my experience, anyone who over-reacts as you are doing usually has something to hide.' He placed his glass down on to the polished mahogany dining-table and propped his chin on his hands, surveying her with gleaming eyes. 'What could your dark secret be, I wonder?'

He was taunting and he didn't have a clue, but it was still more than she could cope with. 'I've had enough of this!' Simone announced, scraping back her chair and standing up. 'You obviously find this all very amusing...' She knew she was going to cry. The tears were there, waiting to well up, to spill over on to her cheeks. She had to get away from him. If she didn't——

'Hey!' He had anticipated her frantic exit, was blocking the doorway out into the hall with amused puzzlement. 'Don't get so uptight!'

'Don't touch me!' Simone stiffened as his hands made contact with her shoulders. 'Let me pass!'

'You're crying—why?' Travis demanded, tipping Simone's chin with firm, uncompromising fingers.

'P-please!' She tried to twist away from his grasp, to avoid staring into the dark, unforgettable eyes.

'Simone, I won't let you out of this room until you tell me!'

It was the first time he had used her Christian name—her *real* one, that was—and it sounded like heaven on his lips.

'For goodness' sake, there's nothing to cry about!' She registered the sudden change of tone, the faint huskiness as the tears spilled with uncontrollable speed on to her cheeks. The shiver of a touch. A gentle hand stroking at the silky golden strands of hair. 'Or is there?'

Simone gulped and took a huge breath, closing her eyes against the cocktail of mixed-up emotions, trembling as each stroke became firmer, lingered a little longer, touched the innermost part of her, the place where a need for sensuous touch still lived, still hoped.

His caress was an oasis in a desert devoid for so long of male companionship. So long since she had allowed a man to get close. So long...

Simone jerked away from him suddenly, frightened by the unexpected responses that were rising with increasing speed through every part of her. 'I can't stay!' she cried wildly, pressing her hands against his broad chest in a futile attempt to make him move. 'Let me pass!' Her voice was unsteady. Blue eyes pleaded.

Travis regarded her reflectively. 'Have I missed something here?' he asked with mild interest. 'A moment ago we were sat down to dinner, having a reasonably intelligent conversation, now you are on the verge of hysteria. What on earth has got into you, Miss Walker? For goodness' sake calm down!' He raised a hand and attempted to wipe away the sheen of wetness, observing her with puzzled, curious eyes when she jerked her head violently away. 'So tell me!'

He still hadn't moved. Not one inch. Standing before her, he surveyed Simone with eyes that dared her to disobey.

'You think I'd tell you anything?' Simone almost yelled. 'You honestly expect me to confide in someone like you?' She beat at his chest in wild anger. 'Let me pass, damn you! Do as I say——!'

His mouth was on hers before she had even finished speaking. No other man would have had the arrogance to stifle such anger with a kiss, Simone reflected with amazed shock, but then Travis Steele was like no other man.

His kiss sent fire running along her veins, scorched her soul, stunned her into subservience. His mouth moved lazily, his hands dragged her close, moulded her against his muscled body.

It had been a long, cold winter. Five years of her life spent suspended in a frozen time-capsule. She had been living a life all these years that wasn't quite real, wasn't quite whole. Just his kiss, his touch and her heart thawed, her body came alive. This was what he could do to her. This was how it had been.

Years older, but no wiser. His power and her weakness. Infinite seconds of utter madness passed as he continued to hold her, continued to move his mouth over hers.

How could she betray herself like this? How could she?

Simone dragged her mouth free, somehow managed to stop herself from stumbling to the ground on legs that felt like jelly, as she found herself released. 'I resign!' she croaked. 'Do you hear me? I resign.' Simone clutched at the handle of the door and then turned, spearing him with a look, hating him a hundred times over for appearing so unmoved, so cool and composed.

He strolled out into the hall after her. 'Not accepted,' he drawled. 'Calm down! There's no need for this overreaction.'

'Don't you dare patronise me!' Simone halted, one foot on the first stair. She was shaking like a leaf, every part of her aware of only one overriding emotion. 'You expect me to work for someone like you?' she cried. 'First thing in the morning, I pack my bags and I leave! Believe me, if I had somewhere to go——'

'Why let something as trivial as that stop you?' The casual expression was gone. Simone saw the dark-angled jaw harden and knew that the line had been crossed.

'Right! I'll leave tonight!' she flared. 'I'll sleep in the car—anything, as long as I don't have to spend another second in your company!'

'No! No! I don't want you to go!' The small wail came from the top of the staircase. Simone looked up and her heart sank like a stone. Jake was standing distraught, clutching his teddy, his eyes large and round with anguish. How long had he been there? How much ranting and raving had he witnessed? Oh, no!

He rushed headlong down the staircase, his tiny feet thumping on each step. 'Don't let her leave, Travis,' he cried. 'Miss Walker's my friend. We do lots of nice things together. She can't go! She can't!'

'If Miss Walker wants to leave, Jake, there's not a lot we can——' Travis began.

It happened so quickly. Simone stood mesmerised for a second as Jake let out a high-pitched wail and then lunged forward down the stairs, arms outstretched. He flew at Travis, kicking and hitting with quite shocking ferocity. 'You mustn't let her go! You mustn't be horrible to her! I like her! She's my friend!'

He was fighting like a demon. Travis stood immobile, deliberately soaking up the jabs and punches, holding the solid body a little away from him. Simone looked on in horror, hardly knowing what to do for the best. 'Jake, stop it!' she pleaded finally, when it was clear his hysteria was mounting, rising inexorably. 'Don't behave this way!' She moved towards him, glancing up at Travis with anguished eyes. 'Jake I... I didn't mean it. Jake! Please! I'll stay! I'll do anything, just stop it!' Her cries didn't make any difference. Jake was quite beyond reason, continuing to lash out with a fury that was shocking in its intensity.

'That's enough, Jake!' Travis's voice was deep and commanding, cutting through Jake's cries with absolute authority. 'You're being very silly.' He lifted him high into his arms and hugged him tightly so that his arms and legs weren't able to inflict any more damage. 'Jake, are you listening? Now stop upsetting yourself.'

'But I don't want Miss Walker to go!' Jake yelled. 'I don't!'

'Calm down now. Miss Walker says she isn't going anywhere,' Travis informed him firmly.

'Are...are you sure?' Jake's tantrum was over as quickly as it had begun. 'Truly?' he sobbed. 'Miss Walker isn't going?'

Travis turned his body so that Jake could see Simone behind him. 'Ask her yourself if you don't believe me.'

Simone moved into his line of vision, saw Travis's grim nod and placed a gentle hand on Jake's arm. She felt the tightness in her throat at the sight of his blotchy face, his tear-filled eyes, and struggled momentarily to speak. 'J-Jake...' Simone gulped and took a breath. She had known, from the first moment of seeing his distraught figure, that she couldn't leave him. 'No, of course I won't,' she assured him. 'I was angry before. I lost my temper. I said things I shouldn't have. I was very foolish.'

Simone glanced into Travis's dark eyes and tried to read the expression that lurked there, failing miserably. 'I was very foolish,' she repeated, looking back at Jake, stroking his plump cheek gently, 'and between now and Christmas I'm going to make up for upsetting you like that. We're going to play lots and lots of games and do lots and lots of exciting things.' Her eyes slid helplessly back to Travis Steele's face.

'Now, Jake, come and have a cold drink of milk. It will make you feel better.' His voice was gruff. With a hard glance at Simone, he carried the child along the hall towards the kitchen.

She felt unbearably desolate watching them go. A wave of loneliness swept over her and she closed her eyes in despair for a moment. So, Simone thought, I'm staying. This is it. My prison. How will I ever cope?

CHAPTER THREE

IT WAS past midnight. Simone hesitated outside the door to Jake's bedroom. She had been trying to get to sleep for ages. But it was no use. The events of the evening were lying too heavily on her mind.

She tapped lightly and then pushed open the door. If she took a quick peek at Jake, just to reassure herself, she would feel better.

Travis was sprawled in a chair by Jake's bed. His jacket had been thrown over the back, shirt-sleeves rolled up, tie loosened. A glass nestled in one hand. Simone saw all this in the time it took to cross the room to Jake's bedside.

'I . . . I just needed to see how he was,' she explained hastily, as Travis raised ebony brows. 'I'm having trouble getting to sleep.' She peered at the peaceful face and felt a surge of relief flow through her as Jake moved in his sleep and momentarily opened his eyes.

'He's OK,' Travis informed her. 'He's having a few bad dreams, I think. That's why he keeps stirring.'

Simone released a small sigh. 'If only he——'

'Hadn't seen you ranting and raving like a mad-woman?' Travis queried with heavy sarcasm. 'Sorry!' he added brusquely, raising his hands in an attitude of apology. 'Sorry. I didn't mean to say that. We were both to blame for things getting a bit out of hand.' He rubbed a hand over the back of his neck. 'I'm tired, I guess.' He looked away, took an almost violent gulp of the liquid in his glass. 'I flew in from New York early this morning, expecting a relatively peaceful day to unwind in, and I come back to——'

'A hysterical governess?' Simone snapped.

Travis shrugged, piercing her with dark unfathomable eyes. 'You said it.'

'You were away a long time,' Simone pointed out, succumbing to an overwhelming need to apportion blame—to make him feel as bad as she did. 'Almost a month,' she added accusingly. 'Jake missed you like mad.'

'You think I don't know that?' His reply was sharp. 'Jake's stoic silence on the other end of the telephone wire, every time I phoned him, practically killed me!'

'You couldn't manage to cut short your trip?' Simone asked, struggling to keep annoyance from her voice. 'Was it so *very* important?'

Travis looked up at her, his gaze unflinching. 'Yes to both queries,' he replied coolly. 'Look, I've worked myself to death, these past few weeks, just so I could clear business out of the way, just so Jake's future would be secure. I don't need you standing here with that pious look upon your face, implying that I've done the wrong thing. Jake's parents died nearly six months ago and I put off everything for most of that time so that I could be with him. But businesses don't run themselves. I had to leave him some time!' He dragged strong fingers angrily through his thick black hair and finished his drink in one violent mouthful. It was obvious he was pretty exhausted. There were dark shadows beneath his eyes, a swarthy growth of beard, which succeeded in making him look even more formidable. 'So if all you're going to do, Miss Walker, is stand there and criticise, I suggest you turn right around and go back through that door, because right at this moment in time I'm too damned tired to argue with you!'

She turned angrily to go, but something, some curious reaction to the stress and the guilt of the past couple of hours, made Simone hesitate as she reached the door. 'Look, if...if you need to rest,' she murmured, spinning back round to face him, 'I could take over here for a few hours. Of course, maybe you prefer to sit beside Jake yourself...' Simone shrugged self-consciously as Travis's eyes traversed the whole length of her body. She had put on her trusty fleece dressing-gown, fastened securely every last button from neck to well below mid-calf, but still, somehow, he could, simply by allowing his gaze to linger, make her feel acutely on edge, stripped of all defences.

'OK.' To her surprise he dragged himself up from the chair and grabbed his jacket. 'If you could stay long enough for me to take a shower?'

Simone nodded. 'Look, about what I said—I didn't mean to——'

'It's OK—forget it!' He shrugged. 'I felt as guilty as hell all the time I was away. You hit upon a very sore point, that's all.'

They were both trying hard. She guessed that Jake's sudden bout of hysteria had shocked Travis almost as much as it had her. He was asleep, of course, and couldn't appreciate their efforts at civility, but then there would be the morning and then the one after that and that...they certainly needed the practice.

He returned in under half an hour, looking...looking completely devastating. I can't go through with this,

Simone thought, glancing away. It's going to be impossible, impossible!

'Is he all right?'

The obscure glow of the night light couldn't hide the fact that beneath the towelling robe Travis Steele was almost sure to be naked. Just one swift, heart-stopping glance on entry had given Simone a glimpse of the broad, well defined chest, the dark matted hair... It didn't take much imagination to visualise the rest.

She jumped up out of the chair as he approached and hurried to the door. 'Fine, just fine,' she breathed.

'I was going to ask if you could hang on for a little while longer, while I go and make some coffee. Would you mind?'

Simone hesitated, then turned and shook her head. 'No. No, of course not.'

He brought in a tray of coffee and sandwiches some while later. Simone had been sitting staring into space for the whole of that time. She almost didn't hear him come in until the last moment, so intent had she been on her thoughts.

Was Travis Steele entitled to some... some sympathy? After all, his sister's death, his brother-in-law too, grieving for them, then taking responsibility for Jake... Simone wavered a little as compassion began to take a hold. No. She shook her head. Any other person and she would have felt enormous sympathy, but Travis Steele? He was a man of cold, hard granite. He could take care of himself.

'Here you go.'

Simone jumped a mile at the sound of Travis's voice close beside her.

'I trust you're not going to react like this every time I come within touching distance,' Travis commented drily, as he set the tray down on to a low table.

Simone licked nervously at her lips and tried in vain to look puzzled. 'P-pardon?'

'Don't waste your time pretending, Simone,' Travis replied with by now familiar bluntness. 'I kissed you and now, it seems, you're practically expecting me to jump on you at every opportunity.' He lifted the coffee-pot and poured out two cups, handing one over to Simone, who took it from him automatically. 'That's what's bothering you, isn't it?' he persisted. 'Look, this obviously needs discussion,' he continued matter-of-factly when Simone turned away from his gaze without a word, 'if you're to stay on here for any length of time. You *are* staying now, I presume?' he added sharply, piercing her with dangerous ebony eyes. 'You did mean what you said? That wasn't just a casual promise you made to Jake? Because if——'

'I meant it!' Simone cut in sharply. She had raised her voice too much. Jake stirred and she glanced over to his bedside guiltily. 'I meant it,' she repeated, lowering her voice, glowering at him from beneath dark lashes. 'Do you really think I would be so cruel as to tell him all that I did without meaning any of it? I feel bad enough about upsetting him, about what happened, as it is!'

'Which makes the two of us,' Travis replied quietly. 'Look, if it's any comfort to you, I don't make a habit of kissing young women in my employ.' He half shook his head, gave a shrug. Both gestures had arrogant devil written all over them. 'It happened. You were angry. I was impulsive.'

'End of story, then!' Simone shot back, striving to look as casual as Travis Steele himself. 'We can forget all about it, then, can't we?'

His mouth turned up lazily and he looked at her with eyes that hardly put Simone's mind to rest. 'Let's just say end of chapter, shall we?' he murmured infuriatingly. 'As I've already said, I'm given to moments of impulse. Who knows what may happen in the future?'

Simone stood up and placed her coffee-cup back on to the tray. What was the point? Sympathy for someone like this? She must have been out of her mind to even consider feeling the tiniest bit of compassion! 'You're damned arrogant, Mr Steele!' Simone replied, fighting to keep an even tone to her voice. 'If you really imagine that I will allow you to lay one finger on me at any time in the future——'

'Simone, you're in danger of becoming uptight again,' Travis drawled, 'and we wouldn't want that, would we? What with your anger and my incurably impulsive nature!' His mouth twisted into a taunting smile and then he had the downright arrogance to yawn and stretch, so that it took all of her powers not to look towards the impressive strength of him. 'When will you learn, Miss Walker? You do bite so incredibly easily!'

She glared and gave a low growl of frustration. What was the use? Travis Steele didn't have a decent bone in his body!

With a look that would have turned a lesser man to stone and a flounce of her fleece dressing-gown, Simone left the room with as much dignity as she could muster.

When she awoke next morning, she knew there was something that was different. She sat up in bed and tried to decide what it was. Something about the room? The light? A certain stillness?

There was a cursory knock at the door and Jake came bounding into the room and she knew immediately what it was.

'It's snowed, Miss Walker!' His face was a picture of the most intense excitement. 'Come and see!' He pulled her arm insistently, virtually dragged her out of bed and across to the window.

It was quite an amazing sight. Everywhere was covered in a blanket of the cleanest, whitest snow imaginable. Perfect. Beautiful. Incredible. Any number of adjectives sprang into Simone's mind as she gazed out, almost as mesmerised as Jake, who pressed his nose against the glass and grinned at the white, white world.

'Can I go out now? Can I? I want to build a snowman. Travis said he would help me. And we can have snowball fights and——'

'I thought your uncle had to go out today?' Simone queried, shivering a little beneath the thin layer of her nightdress.

'I decided against it. Who wants to go to a boring business meeting, when there's all this fun to be had at home?'

Simone looked across sharply to the direction of his voice and found herself blushing furiously.

He was lounging against the open door, casually dressed in black denims and a black cashmere pullover, looking fresh and ruggedly handsome, looking so totally different from how she had come to expect him to be that for a moment she just stared.

And then Simone remembered her own attire and she silently cursed the short silk nightdress, which barely covered anything at all, and dived hastily for her dressing-gown, praying that he would have the decency to look away. She should have known better. Travis's gaze glowed with amused pleasure. 'Would you mind closing the door?' she snapped, as she fumbled her arms into her dressing-gown.

He stepped inside and clicked the door shut.

He was doing it on purpose, Simone thought, just to wind her up. Well, she could do without this at eight-thirty in the morning! 'Oh, very funny!' she snapped, striding across to wrench it back open. 'Now, if you wouldn't mind, I'd like to get dressed!'

'Come on, Jake,' Travis called. 'Miss Walker requires a bit of privacy. I'll see you downstairs for breakfast,' he murmured, turning back to her. 'We can plan the day's events.'

The snowball hit her full in the face and it stung. Simone turned angrily, expecting Travis's demon aim to have been responsible. Instead, she saw an immensely delighted Jake dancing around. 'Got you!' he yelled. 'Right on target!'

Two against one definitely wasn't fair, Simone muttered to herself as she scooped handfuls of fluffy snow like a madwoman and hurled them wildly in the direction of the tree that Jake and Travis were hiding behind.

They had been out for about an hour and Simone was beginning to feel extremely exhausted. She gave up throwing, once her reserves of snowballs had become depleted, and leant back against a tree-trunk, breathing hard. She needed a rest. 'I give in!' she called after a moment. 'You're too good for me!'

Silence. Simone waited and peeped around the tree cautiously.

'Yee-ha!' Jake was beside her on the other side and suddenly she was covered in snow all over again. Simone gasped and wiped it away as quickly as she could, chasing a giggling Jake with a handful of snow.

'Enough now, Jake!' Travis called. 'You need a rest and so does Miss Walker. Go and finish the snowman and then we'll go in and have a hot drink.' Travis came over and joined Simone, sitting beside her on an old tree-stump. 'Here, you've got a great lump of snow stuck in your hair.' He removed his leather gloves and, before Simone could do anything, began to gently tug the ice ball free from the silky strands that tumbled over her parka.

It was agony, keeping still while his hands roamed through her hair. She could feel the warmth of him, the brush of his thigh, clad in tight black denims against her own. She had vowed never to let him get even vaguely close again, and yet here she was—here *they* were, sitting side by side. Simone closed her eyes and waited tensely for his fingers to still.

If he didn't stop soon, she would have to wrench her hair away.

'There; finished. You're hair's pretty wet; you were bombarded unmercifully, weren't you? Do you want to go inside?'

Simone shook her head and put as many inches between them as the tree-stump would allow. 'I'm fine,' she murmured. 'Besides, Jake's enjoying himself so much that I don't want to spoil things.'

Travis gestured at the snow. 'This has made his day.'

'I'm glad,' Simone replied warmly. 'He looks so happy suddenly, almost a different child. Your being here, and the snow——' Simone stopped talking suddenly. It was difficult changing modes. When Jake was within earshot, she spoke to Travis as if they really got on, just for his benefit. But now Jake wasn't in earshot—she didn't have to speak like this.

Simone watched Jake, intent on his task, and felt annoyed with herself. She didn't want Travis Steele to think she had forgiven him for the way he had behaved...

'Thank God children are so resilient. Life—it's hard to fathom sometimes, don't you think?' Travis's eyes settled on Simone's face. 'I used to get so mad with my sister for keeping Jake at a distance, not spending enough time with him.' He shook his head. 'And now, after all that's happened—well, it may just have been for the best.'

Simone turned towards him and frowned. 'Meaning?'

Travis threw her a sardonic smile. 'Let's just say my sister was never a natural born mother. Beautiful, intelligent, but hopelessly bored by children.'

'Even her own?' Simone's voice betrayed her incredulity.

'You find it hard to believe?' Travis queried. 'You think that every mother automatically finds that bonding, that totally overwhelming feeling of love for their child?'

Simone didn't think, she knew. When Katy had been born, when she had held her in her arms for the first time, gazed down at her incredibly tiny face, held the fragile hand... Simone jerked her head away and stared down at the snow. Life *was* hard to fathom. How could she sit here, like this, with *this* man, discussing motherhood of all things?

'My sister just wasn't interested,' he continued. 'She loved Jake in her own way, I suppose, but she didn't make it particularly evident.'

'That's terrible,' Simone breathed, glancing first at Travis and then over to where Jake built in the snow. 'Couldn't she see how lucky she was? He's such a sweet child, so loving—given the opportunity.'

'Depends which way you look at it,' Travis replied casually. 'They say you can't miss what you've never had. If his parents had been the sort that lavished him with affection, spent time with him, then think how he'd be feeling now.'

'That's a rather perverse way of looking at things, isn't it?' Simone asked tautly.

'You think so?' Travis considered a moment and then shrugged. 'Maybe I'm a perverse kind of man.'

'Did you spend any time with Jake—before his parents were killed, I mean?' Simone found herself saying.

'Why do I get the feeling that you expect the answer to be no?' Travis murmured wryly. The corners of his mouth quirked with vague amusement. 'Sorry to disappoint you, but Jake and I have always been quite close. Much to my surprise, I find I like his company. I like most children's company, actually,' he added with evident surprise. 'I've got a couple of friends who have kids and more often than not I find myself spending more time with them than with their parents.'

Simone's eyes held anguish, but he didn't notice. After all, why should he? So he got along with children—no big deal! None at all . . .

'You obviously like your job,' Travis commented. 'I've been watching you with Jake; you're the first teacher he's had who hasn't talked down to him. Why do some people feel they need to do that?'

Silence.

Simone felt a light pattering of snow on her head. 'Anyone there?'

She jerked her eyes to his. 'S-sorry?'

'You're deep in thought,' he remarked. 'Penny for them?'

Simone hesitated, blushing with confusion. She had been thinking about Katy, wasting time on 'might have been's and 'maybe's, knowing full well the pointlessness of such an exercise but indulging in it just the same. One question burned into her mind. She hesitated some more and then decided to go ahead—she was raw enough inside as it was; more pain wouldn't make much difference. 'I was just thinking that I couldn't imagine you with children of your own!' She made her voice sound casual, just the right amount of scorn, the exact degree of disbelief.

'My own? Ah, well, that's a different thing altogether!' He surveyed Jake at play for a moment and then shook his head. 'Consciously bringing children of my own into the world? I don't think so—not for many years yet anyway. Besides which, there happens to be the little matter of a woman. Meaningful relationships have never figured high on my list of priorities——'

'Too busy amassing all this?' Simone cut in, nodding briefly in the direction of the house. She snapped off a twig that was growing pointlessly from the old stump. It's dead, she thought, you're wasting your time! Give up, save your energy!

'Something tells me you don't approve of money,' Travis drawled. 'Too coarse for your liking, is it, Miss Walker?'

She stroked a pound sign in the snow with the twig and then scrubbed it out violently with the toe of her boot, snapping the twig over and over into many tiny little pieces, glad of the almost ferocious occupation.

'The wood's beautiful,' she announced abruptly, getting off the stump, glancing over to the glistening trees. She scattered the broken twigs on to the snow and ground them in with her heel, refusing to pander to weakness any longer.

'We'll take a walk there later, when Jake has had a rest,' Travis declared, 'before the snow goes completely.' He jumped down from the tree-stump. 'But now I think it's time to go inside.

'Looks pretty good, doesn't it? Although I hardly think it's worthy of the amount of attention you're giving it!'

Simone spun around. She had been lost in thought, under cover of admiring the huge fir tree that sparkled so majestically in the corner of the hall.

Travis leaned on the banister and raised ebony brows as Simone looked up at him blankly. 'Quite a thinker, aren't you, Miss Walker? You've been lost in a trance for almost ten minutes. What goes on in that pretty little head, I wonder?'

He was teasing, of course, and he wanted her to bite. She almost did too, but found common sense from somewhere at the very last moment—just in time to see the aggravating curl of a smile at the corners of his mouth. Simone pressed her lips tightly together in annoyance.

'So are you coming?'

She replaced a painted wooden bauble back on to the tree and turned to face him. 'Where?'

'To the wood. Remember you said how lovely it looked, how you wanted to see it? If we don't go soon, it will be dark.'

She had succeeded in avoiding him since late morning—working in the schoolroom, while Jake took a much needed rest, dining in the kitchen with Mrs White—generally keeping out of his way. It couldn't last indefinitely, she supposed. 'I'll just get my coat,' Simone murmured. 'Is Jake outside already?'

He wasn't outside at all. Simone realised that as soon as Travis began striding ahead at a brisk pace. She hung back hesitantly, frantically debating with herself, wondering what sort of game Travis Steele was intent on playing.

'What's the problem?' He turned, strode casually back, threw her a puzzled frown that was almost convincing.

'Where's Jake?' Simone demanded. 'I thought he would be coming.'

Travis looked at her steadily and lifted broad shoulders in a vague shrug. 'He didn't want to come. Mrs White has enticed him into the kitchen again. I think he did a little too much this morning; the attraction of a warm kitchen and one of Mrs White's gooey cakes was too much to resist.' He took hold of her arm and then somehow his hand was in hers and he was leading her towards the wood.

I'm mad, she thought. What am I doing? Her heart was pounding so painfully that she felt sure he had to hear it. She glanced sideways and looked at the carved, assured profile, before extracting her hand from his and thrusting it determinedly into the pocket of her fleece-lined parka.

If he thought she was going to stroll hand in hand with him through the wood then he had another think coming!

Simone gave a spontaneous gasp of delight as they walked in through the trees. It was absolutely magical, truly like a winter wonderland. Snow sparkled in the icy air all around, crunched excitingly underfoot. She slowed to a halt and spun slowly around, trying to imprint the wonderful scene in her mind.

It was a while before she realised that Travis was watching her. He ran one strong finger along a branch and scooped off the snow into the palm of his hand. 'It's pretty special, isn't it?'

Simone nodded nervously, painfully aware of the sudden intensity of his gaze. 'More beautiful than I ever imagined.'

'Which is what I thought, the moment you crept into my office yesterday morning,' Travis drawled, allowing the snow to fall from his fingers. His dark eyes slid to Simone's furious face.

'Stop it!'

'You don't like compliments?' he queried, dark brows raised.

'Not from you!' Simone snapped. 'No!'

'Because you dislike me so very, very much?'

'Got it in one!' She marched ahead at a brisk pace, following the path that led through a sparkling grotto of frosty silver and white. He thinks because I'm here, alone with him like this, I can't resist his company, she thought. Oh, God! What on earth made me come with him in the first place?

'May I ask why?' Travis, much to her dismay, fell into step beside her.

Simone turned and glanced at his face, saw the expected amused expression. He stood out vividly in this white world, she noted, with his dark, dark hair and ebony attire of fitted jeans and padded bomber-style jacket. All black against all white.

I should never have come, Simone thought, as she returned her gaze pointedly to the way ahead, which led deeper and deeper into the wood. I *am* mad.

'You haven't answered my question!'

A brilliant flush stained both her cheeks. 'I just don't like you! Is that so very hard to believe?' she retorted fiercely, angry with the voice inside her head that hinted at things she didn't want to even begin to know about. She marched on, temper increasing the pace of her stride with every step, so that soon she was almost jogging.

'How long do you think you can keep this up for?'

He was still with her, damn him! Simone stopped abruptly and swung around to glare. 'As long as it takes to get you off my back!' she snapped. 'You're determined to make me mad again, aren't you? Well, you've succeeded! So full marks, Mr Steele! Now if you don't mind I'd like to take this walk alone. It's——'

The fall of snow from the canopy of entwined branches overhead covered her completely. She gasped in shock as the soft icy wetness enveloped her head and shoulders, spluttered comically as she drowned in what felt like a whole avalanche of snow.

He laughed, damn him, he laughed and laughed, and, when she'd scooped the snow from her frozen face and glared at him through frost-fringed eyelashes, he was still laughing.

She was so angry that she felt she would burst. Words failed her completely. She stood for ten whole seconds and just fumed and fumed. And then, astonishingly, she felt the corners of her mouth begin to turn up and, as the suddenly infectious sound of Travis's deep laugh continued, her smile broadened uncontrollably and somehow Simone found herself, despite everything, laughing too.

She pulled off her sodden woollen hat and shook out her mane of hair, tipping her head upside-down so that no more particles could go down her back. Laughing quite helplessly now, she brushed the snow from her shoulders and righted herself, flinging back the wet strands. It must have looked incredibly funny, she thought breathlessly; she couldn't blame him for being so amused.

He came towards her as she unzipped her jacket and helped her shake out all the snow, lifting her hair away with one hand while he removed the snow with the other. 'I do so wish Jake had been with us to see you!' he laughed. 'The look on your face!'

The look on *your* face, Simone thought. The vision of him before her, looking so wonderfully relaxed and happy, shocked her into stillness. He looked so incredible. Laughing eyes, wide relaxed mouth, devastating smile. No sternness, no hardened expression, no arrogant smile. There *had* been strain before, she realised suddenly. He was suffering deep inside somewhere, covering up all the grief of his sister's death . . . Now as she watched his face, studied the vision that wasn't the Travis Steele she hated, she felt her whole body ache with longing.

'Simone, don't!'

She tensed. 'Don't what?' she whispered.

'Don't look at me like that, Simone.' His voice was low, suddenly husky. No smile now, just gorgeous gleaming eyes and a predator's look. It pinned her to the spot, took her breath away, removed her instinct for self-preservation.

He still held her hair; she felt the gentle tug as he wound the strands into one thick coil, pulled her head back just a little, so that her face was tilted up to his.

They gazed into each other's eyes for several silent seconds.

'I'm going to make you mad again,' Travis predicted huskily. 'Do you think you can bear it?'

The sudden warmth of his mouth moving hungrily against her lips sent shivers of intense desire through every part of Simone's body. She shuddered uncontrollably as his kiss deepened and he pulled her even closer with a small growl of satisfaction, tugging her hair back some more, kissing her neck, trailing his tongue sensuously along the chilled line of her exposed throat. 'I want you!' The words were breathed erotically against her skin. He repeated the demand again as his lips returned to her mouth with possessive intent, as his tongue deftly probed the moist interior.

On and on. Glorious desire. Simone was powerless beneath his touch as his fingers found the curve of her breasts. He moulded and kneaded, slipping his hand beneath her soft woollen jumper to find the darkened peaks, increasing her need for him with every shocking touch.

Time stood still, reason and thought deserted her as his mouth and his hands seduced her, reduced her to a mindless mass. She felt the release of her hair, his fingers slipping down her back, pressing her against the hardened length of his body. She felt his urgent need of her, was aware as he pushed her back against the broad trunk of a nearby tree that he wanted to take her here and now, wanted to show her how much he desired her.

Both hands were beneath her jumper now, lifting the knitted wool deftly, pinning her pliant arms against the trunk above her head so that she was shockingly exposed, so that he could feast hungry eyes upon her.

She was utterly lost, helpless with need and sexual desire. Five years of celibacy, five years of telling herself that she didn't need anyone, didn't need *him*, had been in vain. He knew, she knew that this need had to be extinguished, right here, right now...

The sudden harsh call of a bird, close at hand, saved her from her fate, saved her from utter degradation.

Simone's eyes flew to where the sound had come from and with a little cry of disgust she wrenched her arms free from Travis's hold.

The bird, startled by Simone's sudden movement, flapped silently away, selecting another perching position that was higher still. Simone glanced up, frantically searching for the black bird, as she hastily rearranged her clothes, zipped her coat, thrust her hat back on to her head. There it was! She stared at it for a moment, and then closed her eyes, desperation etched into every feature.

A raven. There was no mistaking the heavy head, the large stout bill. The bird of ill-omen.

Simone swallowed and stared at Travis with eyes of pain. She didn't know what to say; there were no words that could describe how she felt.

'Don't look at me like that!' he commanded quietly, piercing her with angry eyes. 'You wanted it as much as me. Simone!' He took her by the shoulders and shook her. 'Don't do this to me!' he urged savagely. 'Don't do this to yourself! We both want the same thing! Why fight it?' Simone gazed with unseeing eyes and felt ice replacing the fire in her veins.

'I want to go back.' Her voice was like stone, heavy and cold, incapable of feeling.

She turned and followed the line of tracks that led back to the house, aware, as she walked, of the raven croaking high in the tree-tops.

CHAPTER FOUR

TOO late. Simone glanced for the hundredth time towards the church hall door and felt her hackles rising as Travis Steele made his much longed for appearance.

She looked back towards the stage, concentrating as best she could on the words of the final carol which was being sweetly sung by the whole of the Sunday school, and tried not to look at Jake's trembling bottom lip.

Travis had known about this important event for days now, had been reminded by Jake a hundred times or more. She had even left him a note herself just before they left, prominently placed on his desk, just so that he would have no excuse not to be here on time.

Simone felt her eyes filling with angry tears and hurriedly glanced down at her lap, pretending to read the programme, although quite why she would want to do that, when the performance was at an end . . .

Damn him! How could he do this to Jake? How could he be so insensitive? It had all been for nothing. All the weeks of hard work, the pleasure that Jake had gained from mixing with children of his own age each Sunday—wasted!

Without Travis Steele's prominent figure in the audience, which consisted of scores of adoring parents, grandparents and friends, Jake's much practised few lines had been delivered in only a miserable whisper. It was almost too cruel, Simone thought now, as she cast furious eyes to where Travis Steele stood watching, that he should make an appearance at all. Better surely to miss the whole thing if he couldn't be bothered to turn up for the most important part.

She weaved her way towards the hall door, once the children had been escorted out to another room to get changed and to have a drink, conscious of the lump in her own throat.

There were to be refreshments for the audience—this was quite a social gathering in the tiny village—but Simone really didn't think she could bear it. She harpooned Travis Steele, who was chatting casually to a group of much admiring women, with a look of sheer dislike and let herself out of the double doors.

The snow had lasted for two days. Now, a week later, nothing of it remained. Simone took a gulp of the frosty night air and tried to keep calm. In a moment she would have to rescue Jake, but first she needed to compose herself.

She wrapped her smart woollen coat tight around her and strolled across to the churchyard. The moon was a silvery ball, high up in the inky sky, clearly visible between the blackened branches of the ancient trees, shedding more than enough light to see by.

Her boots crunched noisily on the gravel path, and she could hear the muffled chatter from the hall. No doubt he would be in there now, socialising, drinking coffee and consuming mince pies, or whatever it was they were having, wasting time with people he hardly knew, she thought bitterly.

The feeling of hate contained within her at this very moment shocked her. She felt quite, quite outraged by his totally callous behaviour.

Simone halted in her tracks and then turned around suddenly. Jake needed to go home; he would have changed by now, and staying out here was only prolonging the poor boy's agony.

And then she saw him, a large imposing figure, striding along the path towards her.

She launched into her attack before he had got within six feet of her. 'Well, are you pleased with yourself?' she demanded, glaring at him, refusing to be intimidated by the assured brute force of the man. 'You've succeeded in destroying all the progress that little boy had made—you know that, I suppose! You've succeeded in making him as miserable as hell! I hope you realise that too!'

He had reached her now. Simone stared up into the dangerously dark eyes, and tried to read something into the wooden expression. Was there even a glimmer of remorse, a flicker that showed he was even a little distraught that he had missed Jake's moment of glory? She shook her head with faint disgust and answered her own question as swiftly as it had been posed. No, of course not! What was a Sunday school nativity play to a man like Travis Steele?

'He's probably crying in there,' she continued unsteadily, 'being brave and trying to take your thoughtlessness in his stride, crying quietly to himself, no fuss, no show of histrionics, just silent misery. Did you see his little face when they all filed out? Did you?'

'Have you finished?' His voice was like thunder, low and deep, threatening a storm of abuse at any moment.

Simone took a shaky breath. It had been a week since she had been this close to him, a week in which curt nods and clipped sentences had been their only method of communication. They had avoided each other like the plague. Now, as she stood before his towering frame, she had to fight to keep control. 'Yes,' she replied coldly, 'I have.'

'Well, thank the lord for that!' he snarled. 'Because one more accusatory sentence from you and I may not have been responsible for my actions! Just who the hell do you think you are, launching at me with an hysterical tirade like that?'

'I'm Jake's governess,' Simone retorted urgently, 'and I care what happens to him! I care that tonight he has been hurt unnecessarily by someone who hasn't got a decent bone in his body!'

'By me?' His voice held incredulity.

She knew she had gone too far, but somehow she didn't seem able to stop. All the frustration and anger of the past week just spilled out of her. Night after lonely night she had lain awake and relived the humiliating episode in the wood, torturing herself with the knowledge that Travis Steele still had the power to ruin her life.

'Of course by you!' she stormed. 'You've neglected your responsibilities badly and you know it! Of all the people who most needed to be here tonight...!' She shook her head with incredulous disbelief. 'I just don't understand why you couldn't have made the effort. Surely one night away from your business or your women or whatever it is you were doing wouldn't have been so difficult! In fact——'

'Hold it right there! Don't you dare say another word, lady.'

Simone gulped at the sudden ferocious tone. She stepped back a pace as Travis moved towards her, a look of controlled rage clearly visible on his moonlit face. He moved again, and Simone retreated some more. 'Don't you think I know exactly how I've made Jake feel?' he ground through clenched teeth. 'Don't you think I know how much damage has been done, simply by not getting here on time tonight? Well?'

He had somehow manoeuvred Simone so that now she had her back against the rough stone wall of the church, with no option but to glare up into his dark, incredibly angry face. 'Or do you take me for an idiot, as well as an uncaring bastard?' he continued savagely. He moved in closer still, imprisoning her with his arms. 'I wanted to be here tonight—of course I did! But my life is complicated, Miss Walker; unexpected situations arise, difficulties that weren't even on the horizon two minutes ago set in with frightening speed. If it's within my power I deal with whatever comes up. Some things, however, are beyond my control. That is the case tonight. When I explain to Jake he will understand.'

'You...you think so?' Simone said frostily, determined not to show how easily he could intimidate her.

'He will have to!' he replied tightly. 'But let's get one thing straight, shall we?' he added, and his pitch-black eyes pierced hers with formidable power. 'I know when I've made a mistake—always. The last thing I need, Miss Walker, is an interfering, know-it-all governess pointing out the obvious! So in future you may keep your observations to yourself!' His face was just inches from her own. Simone shut her eyes and tried to swallow, tried to move. She couldn't. 'Have I made myself clear?'

'Get away from me!' she spat frantically.

'Not until you acknowledge all that I've just said!' he replied with insistent venom. 'Do it!'

'Don't you dare talk to me like that!' Simone's eyes flashed open.

'Dare?' he gritted.

She had made a mistake. She knew that the moment she had finished the sentence. In this mood, such a blatant challenge was like pouring more fuel on to an already blazing inferno.

'Try daring me, Simone, and see where it gets you!' he thundered. His mouth covered hers in a brief but fierce, possessive kiss that warned and threatened and promised, and left Simone feeling as weak as a kitten. And then he released her and strode back towards the church hall.

Simone didn't drive back to the house immediately. She just couldn't face it. In fact she doubted if she could ever go back there to work again. It was Christmas in just three days and she had nowhere to go, nothing to look forward to, except the prospect of spending a miserable time trying to steer well clear of Travis Steele, trying to pretend to Jake, who still looked anxiously towards her whenever the three of them were together, that everything was just fine.

Simone pulled her battered yellow Mini into the parking space at the top of the hill and stared miserably through the windscreen at the view of the village down below. Damn it! Money or no money, she would have to get away, even if it was just for Christmas and Boxing Day. But where to go? She sat and stared with unseeing eyes. No family. Friends, but none that she would ever dream of imposing on...

Scrabbling in her glove compartment, she found her trusty supplies. Simone plugged her portable water heater into the cigar lighter, filled a mug with bottled water and coffee and unwrapped a chocolate bar. She wouldn't go back, she would stay here a while, look at the view and think. There had to be a way to get herself out of this mess.

Two hours later and she still hadn't come up with anything. The trouble was, thinking made her miserable and misery prevented her from doing the sensible thing like driving back to the estate before she got frozen to the bone.

She had dozed off—a silly thing to do when the temperature outside was well below freezing, Simone realised as soon as she awoke. Her feet were like ice, her fingers were numb and it took all the will-power in the world to turn the ignition key and head back to the large, imposing mansion.

He would still be up, she knew that, despite it being hours later. Travis Steele seemed able to survive on very little sleep, and the thought of having to face him all over again filled her with dread.

But where else did she have to go? Money had never been a particularly high priority—if she had it, she spent it, and at the moment her funds were at an all-time low, mainly due to the expense of keeping her decrepit old Mini on the road.

Simone shivered as she drove, and wished the heater in the car were more efficient. She felt quite unwell. Frozen to the bone, worn out, miserable. 'I thought I was strong,' she murmured, as she swung the Mini through the impressive high gates that heralded the entrance to the estate. 'I thought I would have the strength to cope with him, to cope with the memories.' She shook her head in disbelief, her voice sounding incredulous in the frigid interior of the car. 'I must have been crazy!'

Simone had negotiated perhaps twenty yards of the tree-lined avenue, in a trance that wasn't far removed from sleep, when two bright, dazzling spots of light appeared from around a bend. For a second she was mesmerised by the sudden glare and then as the fear of a head-on collision became an actual, frightening possibility her reflexes took over and she swerved to the left and slammed her foot hard on to the brakes.

She had been travelling a little too fast, she realised that the second she hit her feet on to the pedals. The tyres skidded on the layers of sodden, rotting leaves that lay along the edges of the drive, and then the wheels locked beneath her and the car slid to a halt just inches from the trunk of a very large and immovable tree.

She was incredibly lucky—not that she appreciated her good fortune much at the time, but later, quite a bit later, she could see how lucky she had been to escape without any injury.

Simone sat slumped over the Mini's large, outdated steering-wheel, breathing a little unsteadily at her narrow escape.

'Do you know how close you were to crushing this heap of rust?' Travis had wrenched open the driver's door and was glaring down at her. 'Where the hell have you been all evening? Jake has been worried sick!'

Simone felt the hot flame of temper rising within her. She jerked her head around and speared him with a look of sheer dislike. 'Do you always drive like a maniac?' she enquired icily. 'I had to swerve like crazy just to avoid you!'

'You were the one smack bang in the middle of the drive!' Travis pointed out coolly. 'Did you know this wreck has only got one headlight working, by the way? You were lucky not to get stopped by the police.'

Simone released a taut breath. She almost wished she had. Perhaps they would have given her a bed for the night—then she wouldn't have had to return to this place! She wrapped the folds of her camel coat more tightly around her, shivering helplessly. It was a beautiful night, she noted belatedly, stars twinkling in the dark velvet sky, the ground, the bare branches of the trees crisp and white with a heavy frost. 'W-would you shut the door?' Simone requested, suddenly weary and feeling hopelessly defeated by the conflicting emotions that tortured her whenever Travis came within a few feet. 'I...I'm cold and tired. I don't need any more aggravation.'

'You're frozen, aren't you?' He reached forward and placed a large warm hand over her frigid fingers. 'Come on. Out you get. I'll take you back to the house in the Rolls.'

'I'm fine!' Simone muttered unsteadily. 'Just leave me alone!'

'Don't be ridiculous, Simone! You're far from fine!' Travis retorted quietly. 'You look as pale as death and you're shaking like a leaf.'

'I...I sat in the car too long,' Simone admitted, in a moment of weakness. 'The heater doesn't work properly.'

Travis bent forward and pulled Simone towards the Rolls without a word. She got in, too cold and tired to protest, and Travis reversed at speed, expertly swinging the car into the courtyard before coming around to help her out again.

'I'm not ill,' Simone protested feebly. 'Just cold. Don't fuss!'

'You're chilled to the bone. Look how violently you're shivering. Here, let me carry you. Your legs look as if they're about to give way beneath you.' He swept her into his arms before Simone had even opened her mouth to protest. She felt strange as he held her close, knowing an almost overwhelming compulsion to lay her head on his shoulder, to close her eyes and sink against the fine woollen cloth of his suit. Oh, dear, she thought dazedly. What on earth is wrong with me? Is it just my body that's frozen or my brain as well?

She felt as weak and as defenceless as a baby. It wasn't easy keeping up the hardened attitude, the defensive stubborn expression when he was holding her this close, this gently. She felt curiously protected with his arms around her body, desperately aware of how wonderful it felt to have this man taking care of her.

He carried her up the stairs and flicked the light on in her bedroom. Tears welled up into her eyes as he laid her carefully on the bed and she hastily turned her head.

I mustn't cry, she thought, I mustn't!

Travis helped her out of her coat. 'How do you feel?' he asked.

'I'm fine,' Simone muttered, closing her eyes, refusing to witness the almost sympathetic expression on his face that made her want to cry even more. 'My. . . my feet are frozen solid and I can't feel the ends of my fingers, but—what are you doing?' she demanded fiercely, as Travis began to remove her black leather boots.

A smile tugged the corners of his mouth. 'What does it look like? Helping to get some circulation going in these icy toes of yours.'

His fingers massaged thoroughly, stroking her skin with firm assurance, sending shivers not of the cold, but of awareness, until Simone could stand the tantalising experience no more. 'I'm all right now. Thank you!' She murmured swiftly, dragging her feet from his hold. 'They feel much better now.'

His mouth curved into a far too knowing smile. 'I'll get you a hot drink. Now get undressed,' he instructed, 'and then into bed quickly. Have you got something warm to wear? Flimsy négligés might increase *my* body temperature but they're not going to do a lot for yours!'

When he returned Simone was still struggling with her dress. She had managed to undo it part of the way, but the zip had got caught in the fabric somehow and was stuck fast.

Travis put down the steaming mug he held on to the bedside table and finished the job in one swift movement. 'Now into your nightdress and then into bed.'

'With...with you in the room?' Simone queried shakily. 'Do I look that stupid?'

'No, but you look pale and cold,' Travis remarked coolly, 'and if you don't get yourself undressed by the time I count to ten, then I'll undertake to do the job myself.' His mouth twisted attractively. 'Go on! Don't worry, I'll turn away at the vital moment!'

She didn't trust him, not one little bit, but then, she thought as she struggled to remove her bra and panties, watching suspiciously as Travis Steele turned his head towards the wall, he hardly fell into the voyeur category. If Travis Steele wanted to see her naked, he wouldn't sneak a view—he'd stand there with complete masculine cool and just look and look.

She was in bed shivering in ten seconds flat.

He sat on the edge of the bed and handed her the mug of scalding tea.

'Now drink and try to relax.'

'There's no need for this,' Simone murmured with defensive chill. 'I'm quite all right!'

'Will you stop saying that?' he drawled. 'Look, you're shaking.' He reached over and tucked the quilt up around her as if she were no more than a child, which was, curiously, how she felt just at that moment. Simone raised the mug to her lips and took a reluctant sip of the over-sweet tea. 'So where were you all evening?' Travis asked, surveying her with piercing ebony eyes. 'Jake was worried.'

But not you, Simone thought bitterly, sipping some more, not you!

'I went for a drive,' she murmured, avoiding his face.

'To cool off? And no,' he added, 'that wasn't intended as a pun.' He waited a moment and when Simone made no reply he said, 'You still haven't forgiven me?'

'Has Jake?'

He looked at her levelly. 'I think so. We were on good terms when I put him to bed this evening.'

'He's a sweet child, he's six.' The desire to goad him was quite overwhelming suddenly. 'You can obviously wind him around your little finger.'

Dark eyes burned into hers. 'I've explained what happened to Jake and he accepted my explanation. If you can't handle that fact, Simone, then that's your problem.'

'Let's just say I'm...I'm not so easily fooled!' Simone retorted tartly. She placed her mug on the bedside table and slid further down under the blankets, trying not to shake too much.

Travis released a sigh that was pure control. 'For goodness' sake! Will you stop acting like a child, Simone?' he commanded. 'You've sulked around the house for the last two days without a word. You storm off after the carol concert and now you're talking like a petulant little girl!'

I must be ill, Simone thought as she laid her head back against the pillow and felt her eyes fill up with tears. I should be bawling at him to get out now, beating my fists on to his chest in anger at the very least. She wanted to howl aloud, wallow in self-pity.

No, she didn't. She wanted someone who loved her dearly, who cared about her more than anyone or anything else in the word, to hold her close, comfort her with words and kisses.

'I'm extremely tired,' she mumbled, turning her face into the pillow so that he shouldn't see her tears. 'It must be very late.'

Travis rose from the bed, clicked off the lamp beside the bed. 'Yes, you're right, Simone,' he murmured in the darkness. 'It's far too late, isn't it?'

'Are you feeling better now, Miss Walker?'

It was the following evening. Simone was ensconced in the drawing-room with Jake at her feet, reading him the story of the nativity. To an outsider's eye, it was the picture of cosy family life: a roaring log fire, rich velvet curtains drawn against the winter gloom, the sparkle of the Christmas tree, presents beneath, frequently rearranged by an inquisitive Jake.

Oh, yes, Simone mused, laying the story book down on her lap for a moment, it was quite an enchanting scene!

She let out a disconsolate sigh. What was happening to her? She was becoming bitter and hateful, twisted and churned up inside, and it frightened her.

'Did you like my singing yesterday?' Jake asked.

'Singing?' Simone glanced down and looked at his face with a blank expression.

'Yes. My Sunday school singing. Travis said I did brilliantly!'

Simone smiled and pushed away the thought that as Travis had hardly heard more than a few bars he was hardly in the best position to judge. 'Oh, yes, sorry, Jake. I wasn't thinking properly. Yes, you sang very well. And you knew all the words. I was very impressed. Very proud of you.'

Jake fiddled with the cord of his dressing-gown for a moment and then looked up into Simone's face. 'You know, Miss Walker, you mustn't be mad with Travis for missing the play,' he informed her seriously. 'He couldn't help it if there was a real live bomb in London and the police and the army were swarming around, could he?'

'A bomb?' Simone glanced down sharply. 'What are you talking about, Jake?'

'It didn't explode,' Jake continued carefully, 'don't worry.'

'It didn't explode?' Simone repeated, her voice rising with every syllable. 'A bomb?'

'No,' Jake replied. 'The army came and deto...deto...'

'Detonated it,' Simone finished automatically.

'Yes, that's right. Travis said I wasn't to worry because he was a long way from it, but all the traffic got jammed up and that was the reason he was late. So you see, Miss Walker, he didn't mean to miss my play. And he was very, very sorry.'

A bomb? Simone leant her head back against the sofa, her whole body sagging suddenly. She bit worriedly at her lip. Travis had been late because of a bomb-scare in London? She closed her eyes for a fraction of a second in despair, remembering the report on the news this morning. Oh, no! All the things she had said to him!

'Jake, do you think you could play quietly for a moment?' Simone murmured, rising swiftly from the sofa after a few moments' thought. 'I just want to have a quiet word with your uncle.'

Jake grinned knowingly. 'OK, Miss Walker!'

'I've come to apologise,' Simone announced quietly, pushing open the door to his study. Travis sat at his desk, staring intently into the screen of his personal computer. 'Jake told me about the bomb-scare.' She hesitated, watching the unmoving yet still dynamic figure with trepidation. 'I . . . I didn't realise.'

He turned his head and gave her a considered look from shrouding eyes that were without expression.

'Look, I . . . I went overboard,' Simone continued jerkily, after it was clear Travis wasn't going to speak. 'I'm sorry, but I was upset at seeing Jake so . . .' Her voice trailed away and she pursed her lips—Travis Steele obviously wasn't about to make things particularly easy for her. He turned back to the screen and continued working. 'Well, is my apology accepted or not?' she asked with sudden irritation. 'I can do no more than say I'm sorry!'

'You've been considering spending Christmas in a hotel,' he said in clipped tones, still surveying the screen.

'Drop the idea and spend the time with us and you will be forgiven.'

'You . . . you've been listening in to my calls!' Simone accused. 'How dare you?'

'I picked up the receiver at an inopportune moment. I can assure you I do not stoop to something as despicable as listening in to other people's phone calls, despite what you so obviously think!' he retorted. 'Well, do you agree to my proposal or not?' He continued almost savagely, 'At the moment Jake is under the impression that you will be around to share in the festivities. Am I to tell him that you prefer an impersonal hotel room to his company?'

'Do you always manipulate people so effectively?' Simone flashed bitterly.

'Of course.' He raised ebony brows and Simone saw impatience creeping into his expression. 'Well?'

She hesitated for a split-second, let out a sigh of annoyance and then nodded. There was only one decent hotel in the near vicinity and its prices were well above what she could afford anyway.

'Good.' His eyes swivelled back to the screen in an infuriating attitude of dismissal and Simone turned back towards the door with an angry grimace. 'By the way, how are you feeling now? No after-effects?' It was a casual enquiry; he didn't even raise his eyes from the precious computer, she noticed.

'Do you honestly care?' Simone retorted stiffly.

'I wouldn't have wasted my breath if I didn't,' he drawled, looking up at her with stunning eyes. 'Come on, don't you think it's about time you relaxed, Simone? Tomorrow is Christmas Eve. It would be nice to think we could reach some sort of truce—for Jake's sake, if not for our own.'

'Jake, Jake! You throw him at me every time, don't you?' Simone stormed.

'Well, for me, then!' he rasped, standing up, his eyes spearing hers. 'Do it for me! I am sick and tired of the atmosphere. Sick and tired of being treated like some sort of evil demon! For goodness' sake, can't we forget what happened? Or are you going to insist on holding it against me for the rest of eternity?'

Simone swallowed, felt her stomach knot into a tight ball. If only he knew! she thought weakly. If only he knew just how dramatically he had altered her life, what she did have to hold against him...

'What happened in the wood, happened,' he continued quietly. 'And I won't apologise, because it felt right and it felt good.' He came around the side of the desk and Simone felt apprehension stir. 'I find you physically attractive, Simone, and I see no reason to deny that fact——'

'Oh, well, that makes everything all right, then, doesn't it?' Simone cut in with deliberate harsh sarcasm. 'I suppose you expect me to feel flattered! After all, powerful Travis Steele, millionaire businessman and womaniser extraordinaire——'

'Womaniser? What the hell are you talking about?' he replied in a clipped voice.

'You know!' Simone cried, shooting him a fierce, embittered glance. 'The sort of man who has a different woman for every night of the week. Who——'

'Don't get clever! I know the meaning of the word, Simone!' he rasped. 'So I'm classed as a womaniser, am

I?' he continued coldly. 'The fact that you're the first woman I've really wanted in years, the——'

Simone affected a sort of strangled half-laugh. 'And you expect me to believe that?' she retorted. 'Oh, come on! There's enough gossip flying around about you and various female partners to fill a book—no, more than that,' she corrected. 'A whole damn library, I should think!'

Travis raised dark brows and his mouth twisted into a rather bored smile. 'You should know by now that gossip is notoriously unreliable.'

'You're telling me all the stories I've heard aren't true?' she demanded shakily, blue eyes flashing.

'I'm saying they're out of date.' His voice was suddenly low, ebony eyes stared unflinchingly into Simone's flushed face.

'I don't believe you,' she whispered.

'Why not?'

'People don't change. They are what they are...' Simone heard the slight tremor in her voice. She took a controlling breath, looked up startled to find him very close.

'Oh, for God's sake!' He moved forward and gripped her by the shoulders in a suddenly savage movement. 'That's rubbish and you know it! What sort of a person were you ten, five years ago? Exactly as you are now?' Travis's jaw tightened. 'I think not.'

Simone felt the blood drain from her face. Five years ago? Why had he asked her that question? Oh, God! Five years ago and her life had been crumbling around her ears. Five years ago and she had been experiencing the trauma of new life and death, condensed into just a few short, horrendous hours. She had been too young to go through that alone. Too young...too frightened... She had needed his strength then, she had needed him... Maybe if her parents hadn't chosen to ignore the fact that she was pregnant, hadn't virtually told her that it was a good thing that her baby had died, she would have been able to cope better. Simone glanced down at her hands; she had twisted them so tightly together that they had gone white.

'What are you thinking about?'

Simone raised her eyes swiftly. His voice held a sudden quiet intenseness that alarmed her more than anything. She hastily released her fingers, smoothing down her blue woollen skirt in a purely nervous manner. 'I...I was just thinking...'

'About five years ago?'

Simone pressed her lips together and managed a nod.

'Not a good time?'

Simone dragged her eyes from his incredibly hypnotic gaze. Oh, you could drown in those eyes, die and go to heaven...

'N-no, not particularly.' Her voice shook with emotion.

'What happened?'

Simone managed a harsh laugh and shook her head. 'You don't really expect me to tell you!' she replied scathingly.

Travis's mouth twisted grimly. Dark eyes gleamed down at her as he appraised her for endless, heart-stopping seconds, but when he finally spoke his voice was flat, expressionless. 'No, Simone. I didn't.'

He turned away and the broad shoulders shrugged with obvious unconcern. 'So are we to have peace and goodwill in this household for Christmas?' he asked, leaning back against the desk with his arms folded. 'Or are you determined to stick with your policy of silence for the foreseeable future?'

I hate you! she yelled silently. I hate you! I hate you!

Simone brought herself up to her full height, stung him with a look of contempt, snatched open the door and left, with as much dignity as she could muster.

CHAPTER FIVE

'I THOUGHT he was never going to go to sleep.' Travis passed Simone on the stairway. 'Are you coming down for a nightcap?'

Simone hesitated. She had been about to go upstairs to her own bedroom, to have a bath and an early night. It might be Christmas Eve, but she didn't feel in the least like celebrating.

'Do you play chess?'

The question came out of the blue, surprising Simone into an unguarded answer. 'Yes.'

'And are you any good?'

'I like to think so,' she murmured, a little irritation creeping into her tone, because he made it sound as if the likelihood of her being anything but hopeless was pretty unthinkable.

'Well, then, how about a game of chess and a nightcap?' His mouth twisted into a teasing, far too attractive smile. 'And I promise I won't sulk if I'm beaten.'

Simone hesitated. Oh, hell! She hated being miserable, she hated the stiff, hard expression that she had to erect whenever he was around. Underneath, somewhere, there was a girl who liked to laugh and enjoy life. An early night in a lonely bedroom on Christmas Eve—was that what she really wanted?

The release of a breath and a swift nod heralded her decision. '*If* you're beaten?' she queried lightly, managing a faint smile.

She hadn't played for ages and she was a bit rusty. He beat her easily on the first game, but by the second she was getting into her stride and on the third her concentration was so good that they had to settle for a draw.

Travis placed the ornate wooden pieces back into their box. They had been playing, Simone realised with a glance at her wristwatch, for almost two hours. 'You were very good,' he remarked. 'Who taught you?'

Simone took a sip of her martini, cradling the cut glass between her hands. 'I taught myself when I was eight,' she murmured, 'from a book.'

She saw him raise dark brows. 'I'm impressed,' he remarked. 'Quite a difficult thing to do. No help from your parents?'

Simone gave a half-smile. 'Mine weren't that kind of parents.'

He snapped the lid shut and regarded her with interest. 'Meaning?'

Simone released a small sigh and gave a little shrug. 'Meaning they were more interested in the television and horse-racing and going out to the pub. Matters of intellect didn't interest them in the slightest.'

'Do I detect bitterness?' Travis remarked quietly.

Simone showed her surprise. 'No, I don't think so. It's not meant anyway. Long ago, when I was younger, I wished they were different.' She gave a wry smile. 'I got a scholarship to a rather good school and I stuck out like a sore thumb. We didn't have a flash car, we didn't live in the right sort of house, or in the right area. I had a pretty hard time from the other girls for a while—you know the sort of thing.' She glanced around the vast room, expensively furnished with various fine *objets d'art*, and raised her eyebrows in dry amusement. 'Well, maybe not,' she amended swiftly.

'You think I've always lived like this?'

'Haven't you?'

Travis's mouth curved. 'Let's just say,' he drawled, taking a mouthful of whisky, 'I've known more modest accommodation.'

She wanted to ask him. She wanted to know everything there was to know about Travis Steele. But of course interest was out of bounds; so was this, really. After yesterday's set-to, Simone had vowed not to utter one more pleasant word.

'So you no longer blame them?'

'My parents?' Simone set her glass down with infinite care on the side-table. 'No. They did their best for me—as they saw it.'

'But you wish things could have been different?'

Simone shrugged. 'It's all in the past. We are what we are——'

'A phrase that sounds familiar,' Travis drawled. 'Now where have I heard that before? Ah, yes.' His mouth twisted into a smile. 'I remember. We were discussing my colourful reputation at the time.'

'Well, it's true,' Simone replied, a trifle fiercely. 'No one can really change themselves. The surface image might get altered from time to time. We might even be convincing as someone else for a short while, but in the end you can't change what's underneath.'

Travis's lips quirked. 'You still believe I'm a rampant womaniser, then?'

'It's not usual for governesses to be seduced in the middle of the wood by their employer, is it?' Simone snapped, shifting uncomfortably on the sofa as his laughing eyes met hers. How could he sit there and say such things? she thought angrily. After all that he had done!

Dark, impenetrable eyes met hers. 'I was under the impression we seduced each other,' Travis commented with absolute cool. 'For some reason you choose to regret what I look upon as a rather pleasant moment of uninhibited passion.' His lips curled. 'So what is it, Simone?' He paused, regarding her with eyes that unnerved her tremendously, that sent flushes of intense awareness all over her body. 'Is this a guilt thing? Do you have a boyfriend? Is that the problem?'

Simone glared at him furiously. A boyfriend? Was that what he really thought? That she had rejected his advances because of guilt? She forced herself to look him straight in the eyes. 'No,' she replied stiffly. 'I do not!'

'Have you *ever* had one?'

He was goading her deliberately now. That he was nearer the truth than he could ever imagine was unnerving to say the least.

Simone wondered, as she rose determinedly from the sofa, why he felt it necessary to taunt her like this. They had been having a reasonably pleasant evening until now. No, more than that, she corrected honestly, it had been enjoyable—almost companionable!

She shook her head almost in disappointment as she turned from him. 'Goodnight, *Mr* Steele,' she said coldly, emphasising the formal address. 'Happy Christmas to you!'

He had risen almost before she had left the sofa, blocking her way with his large, powerful frame. Simone released a breath of frustration and eyed the small line of tortoiseshell buttons on the front of his black polo shirt. 'Would you excuse me?' she retorted frostily.

'Simone! You are not going anywhere! You haven't finished your drink and *we* haven't finished our conversation.'

'You were taunting me!' Simone accused. 'I don't call that a conversation!'

'I'm sorry.'

It was a mistake raising shocked eyes to his face. He was far too close. Stunning ebony eyes fringed with dark, dark lashes stared back at her. She could see the fine creases at the corners of his eyes, laughter-lines near the edges of his mouth. Did he have those five years ago? she wondered. *Had* he changed?

'Come on, sit down,' he insisted smoothly. 'It's Christmas Eve. I don't want us fighting tonight of all nights.'

He took hold of her hand and Simone felt the rushing sensation of awareness streak through her body like a flash of lightning all over again. She swallowed and allowed him to lead her back to the sofa, aware, as he pulled her gently down on the larger of the two, to sit beside him, that her heart was racing fit to burst.

Was this all it took? she wondered. A smile, a flippant apology and the touch of his hand in hers? She shifted deliberately from him, but he was still holding her hand, intent, it seemed, on keeping her beside him.

'C-could you let go of my hand?' Simone croaked, glancing down to where his large tanned fingers encased her own much slender, much paler hand.

'Do I have to?' His voice was deep and incredibly sexy. Simone felt her breath constrict in her throat as he gazed at her with smouldering eyes.

'Y-yes,' she murmured weakly, 'you do.'

He raised her hand then and brought it to his lips, just brushing the soft pale skin with his mouth.

'Please!' Simone heard the sound of clear desperation in her voice, felt the sharp ache in the pit of her stomach as his lips wandered her skin. 'Don't!' He had to release her. As long as they didn't touch, as long as she kept space between them, like an invisible wall of impenetrable glass, she would be all right.

'Simone, there really is no need to look quite so panic-stricken.' He breathed the words against her still-held hand, turned her palm uppermost, stroked the soft skin with the fingers of his other. 'You have a long life line,' he murmured, 'quite distinct.'

'Stop it!' Simone dragged her hand away in an almost frantic gesture. 'Don't touch me like that!'

'Tell me why it should bother you so much.'

Simone perched on the edge of the sofa and stared at the flickering flames of the fire. 'Because I... I don't like you!' she muttered unsteadily. 'I would have thought that much was obvious!'

'But you find me attractive.'

She turned sharply, a look of forced disbelief and incredulity visible in every line of her delicate face. 'You're even more conceited than I thought!' she breathed.

'I just don't believe in playing games, that's all,' Travis drawled. 'You're no more a fool than I am. We're adults, we each take control of our own lives.' His ebony eyes pierced hers. 'You know I would very much like to make love to you.'

She didn't move. Not an inch. All she could think about was how it had been five years ago. How many times had he expertly seduced her then? How many times had he made her weak with glorious passion? By the end of that incredible night she had loved every part of him. Young, innocent Chantelle had lain awake in the quiet, darkened bedroom watching him sleep, watching the angled planes of his face relaxed with unconsciousness, remembering, going over and over in her mind every last moment of their lovemaking, believing in her stupid innocence that somehow, because it had meant something to her, it had to be the same way for him.

She had felt wonderful, in that brief interlude, in those hours that weren't quite night or day, curled up against the strength of his sleeping body. It hadn't felt wrong or dirty—not then, anyway. Later, oh, yes! She had suffered, called herself all kinds of names, but then...

This *was* a nightmare. The thought that perhaps he knew everything about her flashed through Simone's mind. After all he was a very powerful man, and he had gone through her professional life with a fine-tooth comb. Why not her private life too? Perhaps this was some kind of macabre game, or revenge? Had he employed her knowing full well she had been mother to his child? Was he tormenting her in this way just to send her to hell and back?

The blood had drained from her face. She could feel the sickness in the pit of her stomach.

'Simone? What's the matter?' His voice was sharp, rough with sudden urgency.

Funny, she thought abstractedly, how expertly he could feign concern. She scrambled up on legs that suddenly felt like jelly. 'I don't feel well,' she croaked. 'I need to go to the bathroom.'

'Simone——'

'Let me pass!' She wrenched the hand that was placed on her arm violently away and somehow found herself losing balance, falling backwards towards the wide-open grate and the flickering flames of the fire.

His reflexes saved her. In a split-second she felt Travis's arm around her waist, his hand returned to her arm, pulling her forward. 'Simone, for heaven's sake!'

It had been a close call. If he hadn't caught hold of her so quickly she would surely have...

He was still holding her. Simone gazed unsteadily into Travis's face and felt the treacherous sting of tears. She felt as weepy as a child; weak and unsure and afraid before his vibrant commanding figure. She sucked in a whole lungful of air and struggled to find even a shred of composure. She hated Travis. That was all she had to remember. He had ruined her life, he had been responsible for all her misery.

'Don't touch me!' The amount of venom she had managed to inject into just those three words surprised her immensely. She freed herself from his hold and lanced him with a look of the same kind of intensity.

He gave a half-shake of his head, a disbelieving look that only served to increase Simone's expression of dislike. 'Simone, you have one hell of a problem!'

'Because I choose not to fall for your dubious charms?' Simone jeered, 'Don't fool yourself! You——'

He pulled her to him in one swift angry movement, his mouth descending upon hers with all the finesse of someone who was as mad as hell and seeking to prove a point. His lips moved roughly, possessing hers with a violent determination. She felt his tongue probe the moist interior of her mouth, was shockingly aware of desire and a need to respond, as his hands traced a rough passage along the lines of her body. She could feel the muscled hardness of each and every part of him as he pressed her yielding body to him; felt an uncontrollable shiver as one finger traced an intimate path over the tip of her breast, down over the flat plane of her stomach and beyond.

He released her just as Simone reached the point of mindless response, just as her hands had entwined around his neck, as her fingers had threaded their way through the springy black hair. She saw the hard, satisfied expression and humiliation swept over her once again.

'I do believe I've just proved a point!' Travis rasped, standing back. 'Goodnight, Simone. Sweet dreams!'

She didn't want it to be Christmas next morning. All Simone wanted was to lie with her head under the covers and forget.

Jake bounded into her bedroom at just after seven to show her his presents, bounded out again and then returned an hour later, to tell her that she just *had* to get up.

Church in the morning, more presents, a lunch of huge proportions, which Mrs White ate with them, before being driven by Travis to her sister in the next village.

It was very quiet without the hustle and bustle of the rest of the staff. No Mrs White, no chauffeur, no twittery young kitchen assistant, constantly mooning around because Travis had deigned to bestow one of his gorgeous smiles on her. Simone didn't feel comfortable. It hadn't occurred to her that everyone would go off over

Christmas; she had forgotten that most people had families they wanted to spend time with . . .

In the afternoon they played games with Jake. Simone worked as hard as she had ever done in her life to make his day as much fun as possible. She worked even harder at pretending that it made no difference to her to witness Travis Steele being kind and thoughtful and relaxed and funny . . . It was a special day, after all; he was making an effort, that was all. Underneath nothing had changed. He was still an ice-cold calculating rat!

He came and sat on the floor beside Simone, leaning back against the seat of the sofa. They had just finished playing a rather exhausting new game with Jake.

Travis ran strong fingers through his hair and let out a sigh. 'I'm finished!' he confessed. 'Have all children got this boundless energy?' Simone cast him a swift glance and then looked away.

'You're going to have to talk to me some time, Simone,' he drawled. 'It may as well be now.'

'I don't quite see why!' Simone retorted. 'I——' She halted suddenly as an amused smile spread over Travis's face.

'Well, it's a start anyway,' he drawled. 'Come on, Simone. Sulking doesn't suit you.'

'Sulking!' she hissed. 'After the way you treated me——'

Jake came over and knelt down between them. 'You're not cross with each other again, are you?' he asked anxiously. 'You know God wouldn't be very happy if he knew you were arguing today. Everyone's supposed to be kind to each other at Christmas!'

Simone glanced at Travis and then stared down at her hands.

'It's not a real argument, Jake,' Travis told him. 'Miss Walker and I like each other really.' Dark brows were lifted enquiringly as Travis speared her with a warning glance. 'Don't we, Simone?'

What could she say? Jake was breaking her heart with his anxious eyes! How could she successfully explain to a boy of six, when she couldn't even explain things to herself?

She gave a resolute nod and a smile and Jake jumped up, immediately reassured, zipping out of the room with a shout about getting yet another of his new toys.

'Thank you for that at least.'

'I didn't have a great deal of choice, did I?' Simone replied quietly.

'You mean a lot to Jake.' Travis picked up a shiny new toy car. It was a silver Rolls-Royce, Simone noticed, every detail correct. 'He's quite a different little boy since you've been here. I don't think either of us would want to put that in jeopardy, just because we have a few differences.'

'A few differences?' Simone retorted. 'That's an unusual way of putting it!'

'I was angry last evening,' Travis murmured. 'If I hurt you, I'm sorry. But you should know by now that I won't tolerate being spoken to in that way.'

'Least of all by me?' Simone queried bitterly.

Travis gave a short laugh. 'I can't think of one person who would dare speak to me the way you do,' he informed her.

'Is that supposed to be some sort of compliment?'

He considered deliberately. 'Maybe,' he drawled, raising himself from the floor. He strolled over to the fire and added a new log from the neat pile on the grate.

'So do you think Jake will be ready to go back to school when the new term starts? He seems more than ready now.'

'Th-that's just two weeks away,' Simone muttered. 'I didn't realise you were thinking along those lines...' Her voice trailed away and she stared into the fire.

It was a shock. She didn't know quite why, because she had always known that the post was for a temporary period only. She should be feeling relieved, she knew that—like a prisoner with news of her parole.

'When the headteacher suggested I take him out of school for a while, because of his destructive behaviour,' Travis continued, lounging next to her, stretching long legs out towards the now blazing fire, 'I honestly thought he would never be ready or able to go back. His world was in turmoil and he wasn't coping. He went through three governesses before you; were you aware of that?'

Simone nodded vaguely. 'Jake mentioned something.'

'I bet he did, the little devil! He played merry hell with every one of them. So——' he raised enquiring brows '—what do you think? January the tenth, I believe, is the start of the new term.'

'Of course he's missing friends of his own age,' Simone murmured, almost to herself, 'and as he's progressed so well...'

'And as you're keen to move on——' Travis reminded her.

'Oh, yes, yes, of course.' Simone avoided Travis's piercing gaze. 'Yes, he should be fine at school,' she confirmed with a positive nod of her head. 'Once Christmas is over I'll start getting him used to the idea...'

She felt depressed. Oh, no! Why did she feel so utterly depressed? Wasn't this what she wanted? Hadn't she made it perfectly plain that she was staying here under protest? Jake was ready for school, there was no denying that...

'You don't look very happy. Is something troubling you?' Travis demanded.

Simone looked at him jerkily. 'I'll... I'll miss him.'

It was true. It wasn't the *whole* truth, but then she didn't want to think about the other reasons for feeling depressed—they depressed her far too much...

'One of the perils of becoming too attached,' Travis remarked, with all the coolness of one who had never let a little thing like emotion get in the way of anything.

Simone hardened up her act. 'I know that,' she snapped. 'You don't have to go on about it again!'

'Of course you can stay on until you find yourself another post,' Travis drawled, 'and of course it goes without saying that I'll give you a glowing reference.'

'I don't think a reference from you will be necessary,' Simone retorted. 'I'm quite able to obtain posts on my own merit! Now if you'll excuse me——'

'Not just yet, Simone.' Travis reached across and placed his hand on her arm. 'I have something for you.'

Simone glanced across sharply, a small frown of irritation clouding her expression as Travis got up and reached beneath the Christmas tree. What was he doing? she thought despondently as he pulled out a large rectangular box wrapped in finely lined gold paper. Of all the deliberately audacious men!

'Here—a token of my appreciation,' he drawled, watching her reaction with intense amusement.

Simone stared down at the box and just knew he had given her this to make her feel awkward. 'If you're expecting a present from me, I'm afraid you're going to be disappointed!' she said bluntly. 'I gave Jake a gift, but——'

'And very pleased he was too,' Travis put in. 'You shouldn't have spent so much on him.'

'I wanted to! Look,' she added, standing up, 'I'd rather not accept this, if you don't mind.' She held the package out towards him.

'Ah, but I *do* mind!' Travis replied easily. 'Take it. I want you to have it.'

Simone looked into his face. She knew she should just place the parcel calmly down on to the sofa and walk away. That was what she would have done, had any other man given her this present in the same set of circumstances. But, of course, you couldn't separate things. She wouldn't find herself in these nightmarish circumstances with any other man! If she refused again, she knew only too well what would occur. Behind that misleading smile, she could see the gleam of determination...

She expelled a sigh that signified only too well that she would accept the gift on sufferance. The fact that she was more than a little curious to discover what he could possibly have bought her had to be kept hidden.

'Well, aren't you going to open it?' He looked up and his mouth curved into an attractive smile so that Simone found her heart doing unexpected somersaults.

After a moment's hesitation, she carefully pulled off the ribbon and gold wrapping-paper and lifted the lid of the box, layers of tissue paper, and then there was her present.

Simone stared at the midnight-blue silk for several seconds before raising the dress in front of her. It was gorgeous. Beautifully cut, a long elegant skirt, with a halter neck and a back that was non-existent. Her eyes shifted to Travis's face. She half shook her head. 'I don't understand...'

'There's a card in the bottom.' He indicated the box with a casual wave of his hand. 'That explains what it's all about.'

Simone carefully draped the dress across the back of a chair and investigated the layers of tissue again, bringing out a gilt-edged invitation card this time, with her own name clearly printed on it. 'A dinner party?'

'Looks like it!' Travis drawled.

'And you're inviting me?' Simone queried, suspiciously. 'Why?'

Travis shrugged. 'Why not? You're living here. It seemed the logical approach.'

'And this dress?' Simone continued, casting appreciative eyes over the soft silky folds. 'Is that part of your logical approach?'

'It tends to be rather a grand affair,' Travis informed her coolly. 'I didn't expect you to have something suitable.'

She had nothing like this, that was for sure. Simone picked up the garment and carefully began to fold it away. She wasn't sure whether to feel pleased or annoyed. On the one hand he was inviting her to his private party, had gone to the trouble to buy her this incredible creation, but on the other she couldn't help feeling just a little patronised. He had given it with such a casual, throw-away air...

'Your assistant has exceptional taste,' Simone murmured, remembering the very elegant young female who had interviewed her. 'But I'm afraid I can't accept such an expensive gift.'

'Who said anything about my assistant?' Travis replied casually. 'Kara's been away in the Alps, skiing, for the past two weeks. I spotted this myself on a trip to London. So let's cut the "I can't accept this" rubbish, shall we? I bought it as a gift, a way of thanks for all your hard work with Jake.'

'Oh, I see.' Simone suddenly felt rather ungrateful. 'Well, in that case, thank you. I'll go and hang it upstairs so that it doesn't crease.'

The rest of the afternoon and early evening was spent in entertaining Jake. Once he had been bathed and read a story and tucked into bed, Simone didn't quite know what to do with herself. She meandered into her bedroom, took another look at the dress and then cast a critical eye over her reflection in the wardrobe mirror. Dressed as she was in burgundy corduroy trousers and a baggy, patterned jumper, it was difficult to reconcile the two images. She traced the plunging neckline and shook her head despondently. Lovely as it was, she knew it just wasn't her. Since that night when Jenny and the girls had somehow managed to convince her into a short black number that had left little to the imagination Simone had lived in loose, baggy, practical outfits. This was far too glamorous, far too eye-catching.

Simone closed the wardrobe door. She wouldn't have the nerve to wear such a dress, not in a room full of strangers and certainly not in front of Travis Steele.

* * *

She had washed and tidied the kitchen and was just putting away the last of the clean crockery when Travis came in.

'What do you think you're doing?'

Simone turned, aware of the annoyance in his voice. 'Just tidying around,' she replied hesitantly. 'I didn't want Mrs White to come back to too much of a mess.'

'Mrs White returns tomorrow with an army of helpers,' Travis informed her, casting grim eyes over the freshly washed floor. His gaze shifted to a pile of freshly ironed clothes. 'Did you do that as well?' he demanded.

'I wanted to!' Simone retorted, refusing to be intimidated by his expression. 'It's just a few of Jake's things. I saw them in the laundry-room. I like to keep busy!' she insisted. 'There's no harm in that, surely!'

'Washing and scrubbing and ironing on Christmas Day?' he queried. 'What is it with you, Simone? I wonder sometimes if you don't do things like this to deliberately annoy me! Now shut that damn cupboard door and come with me!'

She didn't dare disobey him. More than anything Simone was aware that the two of them, apart from a sleeping Jake, of course, were alone in the house.

She followed him nervously down the hall, up the small flight of stairs, which separated the kitchen and service rooms from the rest of the house, and into the drawing-room.

'Now sit down,' he ordered, 'and I will get you some supper and a drink. What would you like?'

'Look—Travis.' His name still felt strange on her lips, too intimate; she had to almost force herself to use it. 'I'm fine, really——'

He obviously wasn't prepared to discuss the matter. He poured her a drink, handed it to her without a word and then disappeared from the room. When he returned, he was carrying a tray laden with plates piled high with a variety of delicious-looking delicacies.

'Now we'll eat and then what would you like to do? There's chess, or there's a film on the television which looks OK, or we could just talk.'

Simone considered swiftly and decided in a split-second that the television was the best bet. Talking was too dangerous; playing chess with him somehow conjured up a kind of closeness... 'The film?' she ventured. It was good. A tense thriller that had been a very big hit at the cinema a couple of years back.

Simone, at first too aware of Travis Steele lounging with complete ease beside her on the sofa, had difficulty in concentrating, but soon the well structured plot and excellent acting took a hold and she was caught up in the storyline.

Nerves of steel had never been something Simone could boast about—even the mildest of horror films had her diving for the cushions, so when the crazed madman began stalking the far too vulnerable heroine it was all Simone could do to stay in her seat. She watched with petrified fascination as the tension mounted inexorably, gripping the arm of the sofa, squeezing her eyes shut tight as the killer continued to make his move. The climax was deliberately disturbing. If Simone hadn't had the rugged frame of Travis Steele beside her, she doubted she would have had the nerve to continue watching alone.

When the film came to an end Simone relaxed back against the sofa and released a sigh of relief.

'Well, I don't think I've ever spent a more entertaining hour and a half,' Travis drawled, getting up to switch off the set. 'Watching your face during some of those scenes was absolutely hilarious!'

'Oh, well, I'm glad I'm such a source of amusement!' Simone replied haughtily.

'You've got some imagination!' Travis remarked. 'You were there, weren't you, being stalked by the madman?'

Simone nodded ruefully and stood up. 'Well, yes, I suppose I was. I never dare watch something like that on my own. I frighten myself half to death for nights afterwards.' She stifled a yawn and moved towards the door. 'W-well,' she began awkwardly, 'I think I'll go up to my room now. Goodnight.'

White teeth flashed against tanned skin. 'Better be careful the bogyman doesn't get you, Simone,' he called. 'Remember I'm only along the corridor if you need me!'

CHAPTER SIX

SHE wasn't sure what it was that woke her in the night. An owl perhaps, or the wind that was howling around the house?

Simone lay on her back in the darkness and listened. Nothing. She closed her eyes and turned over, pulling the duvet close around her shoulders. Go to sleep, Simone, she told herself, it's only three in the morning.

She lay still for several minutes and was just beginning to drift back off into oblivion when a thought struck her. The iron. Had she turned it off? Her eyes flashed open and she stared into the darkness, trying to think back. It had been tipped up, she could remember that—she hadn't left it face down on the board or anything, but had she flicked the switch?

Simone let out a breath of frustration. Oh, no! She couldn't remember! And that meant she was going to have to go all the way down now, just to put her mind at rest.

She closed her eyes again for a moment, hoping the worry would go away, and then when it didn't let out a sigh of irritation, threw back the bedclothes and groped her feet into her slippers.

Everywhere was exceptionally dark when Simone opened her bedroom door. She crept along the wide corridor and could just make out the comforting glow of Jake's night light from beneath his closed door. She didn't dare turn on the main lights just yet, not until she had passed by Travis's room at the top of the stairway; his parting words last night were still too fresh in her mind.

She shivered a little as her feet found the by now familiar route downstairs and wished her trusty fleece dressing-gown wasn't still in the laundry-room waiting to be washed—matching négligés were all very well, but they didn't have quite the same degree of warmth.

It wasn't that she liked to frighten herself, Simone thought, as she crept down the short flight of stairs which led to the kitchen, aware that the first stirrings of apprehension were beginning to take a hold, just that she didn't seem able to keep a hold on her imagination. After all, wasn't this house on a par with the one in the film? And hadn't the killer been waiting for his victim in the kitchen, with a rather large and brutal carving knife held high in one hand?

Simone gulped as her mind swung unmercifully back and then she flicked on every single light she could find. If it hadn't been for the fact that she thought she smelled burning of some sort, she would have turned on her heels and fled.

Stop it! she admonished silently, as panic began to rise. You are being utterly ridiculous!

With a great deal of effort, Simone marched resolutely towards the kitchen door and opened it wide before she could frighten herself any more. Nothing. It all looked absolutely normal. Just the laundry door now, check the iron was safely turned off and then back to bed.

It took quite a bit of effort to cross the huge kitchen. She could hear the sound of the wind howling even louder outside, see the black night through the uncurtained windows.

The iron was fine—still plugged in at the socket, mind you, but quite safe. Simone released a sigh, reached up and removed the plug, deciding that as she was here she had better put the ironing-board away too. Mrs White was a stickler for tidiness, especially in this, her very own domain. She wouldn't take too kindly to finding Simone had been in, messing up her laundry equipment.

It was then that she heard the noise. She stood perfectly still, the half-collapsed ironing-board still held in her hands, and listened, every nerve-ending in her body alert. There it was. A sort of distinct scraping, scratching sound, coming from the glass panel in the door that led to the garden courtyard.

The stirrings of panic returned and Simone's imagination did its worst. Was there someone outside, trying to get in? After all, this was just the sort of place to be burgled, with so many objects worth thousands of pounds upstairs. She listened again. Perhaps not a burglar, perhaps someone else. She gulped and felt the hot prickle of fear at the back of her neck. If it were a psychopath she wouldn't stand a chance.

Something caught her eyes, a shadow flashed across the frosted panel and then all the lights went out together and Simone gave a scream, dropped the ironing-board, fell over it and ran like a madwoman from the room. When she collided with a broad, rugged frame at the bottom of the stairs, she yelled some more and fled in the opposite direction.

'Simone! What on earth is going on?'

It was Travis. Of course. Thank goodness!

Simone retraced her steps in the inky darkness and collided with him all over again, clutching at his towelling robe, half sobbing with ridiculous relief. 'There's someone outside, around the back of the house, trying to get in. I heard a noise and then I saw a shadowy figure,' Simone explained breathlessly. 'Please, Travis! Phone the police.'

'Simone, calm down!' His voice was deep, holding all the inherent superiority that was usually so aggravating. He held her close for a moment, pressing her against his solid, masculine frame, allowing Simone the luxury of clinging like a woman possessed, and then he took her firmly by the shoulders and gave her a little shake. 'Take a hold of yourself,' he commanded, 'and tell me slowly what on earth this is all about. I heard a scream and a clatter and I find you running around like a demented hen as if you've just escaped from the clutches of a mad axe-man or something.'

Simone shuddered with feeling. 'Don't say that!' she whispered.

'It was meant to be a joke.'

'This is no time for comedy!' Simone cried. 'The lights have all been turned off! I came down to see if the iron was safe and then I heard something and saw...' Her voice trailed away.

'Saw what exactly?'

Simone hesitated in the pitch-black hallway, aware that while Travis's hands were placed firmly on her shoulders she had no need to feel afraid—although quite how he would defend them both against a mad axe-man she had no idea. 'I...I'm not sure. I thought...I mean there *was* something...'

'Are you sure all this hysteria isn't just the product of a vivid imagination?' Travis asked with obvious scepticism.

'How do you explain the lights?' she hissed worriedly. 'They don't just go out by themselves.'

'Well, I had rather imagined the wind had something to do with it. We have quite a vulnerable series of wires—they're often being knocked out.' He took hold of her hand in the darkness and warmth flooded through her. 'Come on, I'll get a torch. We'll check out your mad axe-man anyway, shall we?'

He led the way and Simone followed blindly behind. When he extracted a torch from a cupboard in the hall everything became worse somehow. It had been easier in the absolute darkness before; now the yellow beam of light threw blackened shadows on to the walls, made innocent things look quite menacing.

Simone held her breath, her eyes darting from side to side, half expecting to see the dramatic silhouette of a raised hand gripping a knife in front of him.

Travis confidently investigated the laundry-room. 'Looks fine to me,' he murmured. 'Wait here.' He stepped over the collapsed ironing-board. 'I'll have a look outside.'

'But...but is that wise?' Simone asked worriedly. 'I mean, if there's someone out there...'

Travis briefly shone the torch in Simone's direction. 'Simone, I honestly don't think you have anything to worry about. You can hear the wind getting up. You probably just heard a branch scraping against something.'

Simone wished she hadn't watched that film. It was terrifying standing in the darkness, watching Travis approach the door, not sure which was worst—that someone could so easily lunge at him outside, or creep up in the dark and attack her from behind.

He was just crouching down, drawing back the lower bolts, when there was a dreadful crash and something smashed into the door, breaking the panel of glass.

Simone, in that heart-stopping moment, honestly thought she would die of fright. She screamed and clasped her hands over her mouth, watching in horror as shards of glass showered into the room.

It was a metal dustbin lid blown up by the wind that had done the damage. Simone saw it as Travis spun around shining the torch on to the floor and ran forward in shaky relief.

'Simone, for God's sake stay where you are!' Travis commanded instantly. 'You'll cut your feet to shreds otherwise.'

'Are... are you all right?' she asked shakily.

'I'm fine. Don't worry.'

'That's easier said than done!' Simone shot back nervously.

It was becoming very chilly in the room now. The wind was gusting through the broken pane. Simone shivered and prayed that the lights would come on again soon. 'Travis, please be careful!' she warned urgently, as he crossed the floor to pick up the dustbin lid. 'There's glass everywhere!'

She heard a muttered curse and knew that he had cut himself. 'There's a broom in that far cupboard by the door,' he said. 'Can you manage to get it for me?'

He directed the beam of light into the far corner and Simone got it for him, holding the torch while he swept the broken glass into a pile.

'I'm going to have to board this up with something and it's going to take a little while. Can you go upstairs and make sure Jake's all right? If he wakes up without any lights he'll be frightened. There's another torch in one of the sheds—you take this one, OK?'

She didn't feel particularly OK—not about going all the way back upstairs alone, even with the torch. 'Do...do you think the lights will be on soon?' she asked, trying hard not to sound like a frightened child.

'You'll be all right,' Travis assured her, as he handed her the flashlight. 'It was only the wind—no mad axe-man.'

Simone left him and crept nervously back upstairs. When she looked in on Jake, he was still sound asleep, despite the fact that the howl of the wind had increased quite dramatically. Simone sat in his room for a while, trying to decide whether to pluck up some more courage, to go back downstairs to see how Travis was getting on. It surely couldn't be very easy boarding up the gap without any help and no real light to see by, she thought.

The door opened just as she had decided to go back downstairs and Travis appeared.

'Jake's fine,' Simone murmured as he glanced across. 'He hasn't stirred once. Did you manage to fix the door?'

'I pinned up some hardboard—it will do for the rest of tonight. Can you leave your torch on in here? I don't expect Jake will wake until morning, but just in case.'

Simone followed him out on to the landing and heard him mutter another curse beneath his breath as he handed her the torch. 'What's wrong?'

'I think I must have some glass caught in my robe somewhere,' he murmured. 'Something keeps digging into me.'

Simone swiftly shone the torch over Travis's body and gasped as quite large shards of glass, caught in the towelling fabric, became visible. 'Travis, you're absolutely covered,' she cried, taking a pace forward to examine his back more closely. 'No wonder you're in pain! There's blood all over your shoulders. Quick! Get your robe off!' Simone instructed.

'Now?' Travis queried.

'Yes. For goodness' sake! Do you want to bleed to death or something?'

It was only when he had slipped the gown to the floor and Simone was hurriedly examining his blood-smeared back, under the light of the torch for signs of imbedded glass, that she realised he had nothing on underneath at all. Her eyes slid cautiously down, following the length of his spine... a little lower and then quickly up again as taut, well muscled buttocks came into view.

'You've got nothing on!' she whispered.

'You've noticed!' His tone held quite obvious amusement. 'Don't sound so shocked. After all, you were the one who told me to strip straight away!'

'I didn't know you were naked beneath the robe!' Simone retorted indignantly. 'I was just thinking about the glass. Your back's in a real mess, you know!'

He turned to face her and Simone raised the torch with a jerk, keeping her eyes and the beam of light fixed high up on his chest.

He wasn't in the least bit embarrassed.

She swallowed and looked into his face and prayed that the lights wouldn't suddenly come on. 'Your bedroom or mine?' Travis asked smoothly, his lips quirking into a smile.

Simone gulped again. 'Pardon?'

'To tend my wounds,' he explained, white teeth flashing in amusement. 'There must be some glass stuck in somewhere—I'm in quite a lot of pain.' Simone eyed him suspiciously. 'I promise I'm not lying, Miss Walker,' he added swiftly, holding up one hand. 'Cross my heart!'

She didn't know whether to believe him or not. She hesitated, remembering the amount of blood she had seen. He had to be in some pain, she thought, and as it was his back there really wasn't much he could do by himself. 'If you get some clothes on, I'll see what I can do,' Simone replied primly, 'but if you think I'm going to help you as you are...!' She thrust the torch back into his hands. 'Here; I'll go and find some cotton wool.'

Simone had pulled back the curtains in her bedroom and was just rummaging in the drawer of her dressing-table, aided by the light of a very watery full moon, when Travis entered.

She felt her heart turn right over, her legs go weak at the very sight of him. He had boxer shorts on this time—nothing else. She watched as he crossed the room, found her eyes surveying the sculptured chest with its mat of dark hair...

'Where do you want me?'

He was teasing. Simone, after a steadying breath, suggested he lie face down on the bed. 'If you could give me the torch,' she murmured faintly. She brought through a bowl of warm water from the bathroom, laced with just a little disinfectant, and set it nervously down on the bedside table. 'I've got some tweezers,' she murmured. 'The trouble is I'm not sure how much I'll be able to do in this light.'

'Do your best,' Travis drawled, turning his face on the pillow to look at her. 'You can always examine me again in the morning, can't you?'

His back was obviously giving him quite a lot of pain. Simone wiped as gently as she could, removing most of the blood, several pieces of glass, but it was clear there were still tiny fragments imbedded in the smooth, tanned skin of his back.

'I'm sorry,' Simone murmured, desperate as Travis flinched silently again, 'but I can hardly see what I'm doing. Do you suppose the lights will stay off all night?'

They came back on just as she had finished speaking. It was quite a shock. Travis propped himself up on one elbow and Simone hastily shifted her gaze. His mouth curled seductively. 'No need to be frightened any more, Simone.'

Who are you kidding? she thought desperately as she picked up the tweezers and prepared to extract a difficult piece of glass. Just seeing him stretched half naked like this on her bed was bad enough; having to actually place her hands on his back, having to stroke and touch and bring her own body so close to his as she worked . . .

'There, I think that's it. I can't see any more pieces.' Simone set the tweezers down and then yawned, rubbing at her aching neck.

'You look tired.' Travis propped himself on to his side and surveyed Simone's pale face.

'Aren't you?'

'Not at this exact moment in time, no,' he murmured softly, piercing her with eyes that halted the breath in her throat. 'Here, let me.' He knelt up on the bed and positioned himself behind Simone.

'What are . . . are you doing?' Simone croaked.

'What does it look like?' Travis drawled. 'I'm repaying a little of your good work with some of my own. Just relax, Simone; your neck muscles are as tight as hell.'

His hands were like fire, scorching their way through the translucent layers of Simone's négligé, melting her resistance with each commanding stroke. Every nerve-end in her body burned with awareness as his powerful fingers slowly moved across her shoulders, pressing and teasing the skin, up towards the long slender neck, back again, and again...

Shivers ran down her spine and his fingers followed the flow of movement. This was ecstasy and agony all rolled into one. Simone knew that what she was allowing him to do was dangerous and incredibly foolish, but when he touched her like this, when she felt the commanding, mesmerising touch of his hands...

Simone closed her eyes and struggled against the weakness of desire as his fingers trailed a path, leaving no part of her back untraced, wondering where his hands would roam next.

He took his time, and then Simone felt the moist warmth of his mouth against the sensitive place at the base of her neck and she shuddered involuntarily, her breathing accelerating as his hands dragged the flimsy lace of her négligé away from her shoulders, revealing silken skin that glowed in the warmly lit room.

His hands were slow, moving across the flat plane of her stomach, teasing with their reluctance to do anything more than lightly explore the outer expanse of silk and lace.

Please! She almost pleaded aloud. She wanted him to touch her. She wanted him to kiss her, to possess her.

Five years and nothing had changed. Five long, lonely years... Looking back over the mists of time, it had been easy to forget how it had really been, more convenient. Simone had chosen to call herself a tramp, a fool, any number of hateful names. Now, with his body close to hers, with his hands lightly exploring every part of her, the memory of how it had really felt to be touched by such a man, by *this* man, came flooding back.

'Mmm, you smell beautiful.' He breathed the words against her neck, tugging playfully at the skin with his teeth, running the tip of his tongue along the line of her shoulder, moving the neckline of her nightdress a little lower, so that the full curve of her breasts was exposed. 'You have a wonderful body, Simone—why insist on hiding it away as you do?' It wasn't hidden now. Simone lowered her head and watched as he traced a gentle finger along the edge of the fabric. Did he know he was driving her crazy? Did he know just how much she longed to feel the male hardness of his body pressed against her own?

She wanted him and for some reason the thought didn't fill her with shame—it should have done, but it didn't... it didn't.

He pulled her back against the strength of his bare chest and Simone tipped her face up and looked into his eyes. Such wonderful dark pools, smouldering with desire, mirroring her own reflection. Simone gazed into the glossy pupils and saw the vision of a woman she didn't recognise, a woman who had lost her senses, and was in acute danger of losing so much more than that if she allowed this expert seduction to continue for a moment longer.

With an agonised gasp, Simone dragged herself free and scrambled from the bed, dragging her nightdress back to its proper position. She stared at him for a moment without speaking, her breathing ragged in her throat and then she lowered her head and covered her face with her hands. 'Please go,' she pleaded. 'Please just go!'

'Simone! What's the matter?' He expelled a long shuddering breath and gave a slight shake of his head. 'What is it?' He came over to her in a flash and Simone could feel the trembling in his body as he gripped her by the shoulders, the frustrated disbelief coursing through his veins.

'Don't touch me!' she whispered, back away from him. 'I... I didn't mean to... Look, I'm sorry. None of that should have happened——'

'What are you saying? Why shouldn't it have happened?' His stunning dark eyes were narrowed angrily. 'Just what sort of a hellish game are you playing here, eh?'

Simone raised astonished blue eyes. She shook her head, her trembling mouth parted as if to speak. But there were no words; she couldn't think of one single thing to say that would make Travis Steele understand. Sexual satisfaction, or rather the lack of it, was all he cared about, so how could she even begin to explain the torment that was running through her at this very moment? 'It's... it's not like that——' she began.

'Not like what?' Travis flashed. 'Do you enjoy bringing a man to his knees and then suddenly—whoosh!—on comes the cold tap?'

'How can you say that?' Simone gasped. 'You——'

'Quite easily,' he rasped, cutting her dead. 'Is it the power you like? You know, I would never have taken you for a tease, Simone—not in a million years. But then what do I know?' He threw her a look that made her blood run cold. 'It takes all sorts, doesn't it?'

'I'm... I'm not a tease!' Simone almost yelled. 'How dare you say that to me? After all that you've done—all that I've gone through!'

'What the hell are you talking about now?' he rasped, shaking his head. 'All that you've gone through! You make it sound like torture of the worst kind. Perhaps I'm not quite with it, but I was under the impression that there was more than a little evidence of enjoyment on your part just now!'

'That's not... not true!' It was. But she couldn't face it. Couldn't admit it to him. She had been so close to giving everything away! Simone's mouth trembled and she pressed the back of her hand against her quivering lips. Why couldn't she learn? Why couldn't she see that nothing had changed? Travis Steele wanted her for one reason and one reason only! Why did she persist in humiliating herself like this?

'You... you took advantage of me!'

He gave a harsh, disbelieving laugh. 'You were positively aching for sex!' he taunted, pausing to spear her with a look. 'And you know it!'

'You bastard!' Simone's whole body shook with rage. 'You cold, callous bastard!' She turned and fled to the *en suite* bathroom, slamming the door shut and locking it behind her.

Tears of misery welled up in her eyes and trickled slowly on to her flushed cheeks. She didn't want to think, she didn't want to feel. She had wanted him and he knew it and the thought filled her with absolute shame. She crossed to the basin and turned on the gold taps, splashing her face with cold, cold water.

She hadn't learned. Five weeks or five years—nothing, it seemed, changed. She was still completely incapable of resisting Travis Steele—and he knew it.

CHAPTER SEVEN

SIMONE sat on the window-seat in her bedroom and watched as yet another set of car lights swept into the courtyard.

She had barely been out of her bedroom all day, lying in bed with thoughts that kept haunting her until almost lunchtime, then creeping down, after she had seen Travis and Jake go off somewhere, to grab a plate of food from the frantically busy kitchen.

The house was a hive of activity, with Mrs White at its hub. She had obviously been preparing for days prior to Christmas. Trayfuls of food were produced from the deep freezes, bottles and bottles of champagne were lined up ready, and she was in her absolute element, organising young Minnie, the kitchen help, who seemed as excited at the prospect of the grand dinner party as if she were a guest herself. 'You lucky thing!' she'd told Simone in her soft country burr. 'Oh, I wish I was going to be wining and dining with Mr Steele tonight!'

She wasn't going to attend, of course, but she hadn't told Minnie that. She'd just murmured something noncommittal about hoping her headache would be gone by this evening.

I'm a coward, Simone had thought irritably as she carried her food back to her room. If I'm frightened to death to tell Minnie and Mrs White there'll be one less for dinner tonight, how on earth am I going to pluck up enough courage to tell Travis?

But then, surely, after what had gone on between them last night, he wouldn't even expect her to show her face? To dress up and don the midnight-blue silk, descend the stairs as if nothing had happened? Simone released a sigh now and shook her head worriedly. Surely not? Travis Steele wouldn't expect her to do that, would he?

It was clearly an exclusive guest list and, as the occupants of the Porsche and Jaguars and Ferraris parked their vehicles and emerged, it was clear that it was a richly glamorous one as well.

How many of them? Simone tried to work it out. Ten, maybe twelve couples? So many beautiful women, so many sharp, well dressed men. She knew, of course, that Travis inhabited a world that was as far removed from hers as it was possible to be. She knew he was unbelievably rich, owned homes in various places around the world; she knew that power and control were as familiar to him as low self-esteem and weakness were to her. But suddenly, seeing these affluent guests, witnessing the grand preparation, she realised just how foolish, how pathetically insignificant she must really seem to him.

She was no more than a rather interesting diversion—a bonus during the Christmas holidays, someone to taunt, to play games with. She had been no more than a plaything five years ago and nothing had changed.

Simone bit despondently at her lip and wondered if it was possible to feel any more depressed than she did now. Her self-image had never been high; now it was at an all-time low.

He had booked a string quartet for the evening, paying goodness knew what rates to secure them on Boxing Night. Simone leant her face against the window-pane, welcoming the coolness on her flushed cheek, and listened to the beautiful melodious sound floating up from the ballroom.

A knock at the door made her instantly alert. Hesitant blue eyes looked towards the sound as her breath stilled in her throat. Was it him, come to ask why she wasn't downstairs? she wondered nervously.

Simone pulled the belt of her towelling robe tightly around her waist and hastened to the door, opening it with trembling hands.

It was Jake.

'Are you all right, Miss Walker? I haven't seen you all day!' His tone was indignant. 'Travis said I could stay up and see all his friends, but that's boring. I want you to read me a story instead.'

Simone heaved a sigh of relief, murmuring something about feeling much better, and took his hand. They padded across the corridor to Jake's room together.

She spent a welcome half an hour losing herself in fairy-tales and nursery rhymes and then, after kissing a sleepy Jake goodnight and shutting his door very quietly, she ventured towards the top of the stairs and peered down at the scene in the hall below.

Travis, dark and dynamic, dressed in immaculate evening attire, was greeting some late arrivals. Simone took a hasty step backwards into the depths of shadow and watched as two people came in through the large double doors.

He was saying something amusing to a tall, elegant brunette and he looked so superbly handsome, so overwhelmingly incredible that Simone found herself trembling just at the very sight of him. How could he do this to her? How could he make her feel so churned up inside, so compelled?

There was a peal of laughter from the young woman and Simone watched intently, trying desperately hard to ignore the feeling inside that seemed distinctly like jealousy, as Travis wound his arm casually around her waist, whispered something close to her ear and led her off towards the drawing-room.

She leant back against the wall and let out a shaky sigh. Why put herself through this torture? She didn't want to be here! She didn't want to have to even think about Travis Steele ever again...

'What are you doing up here?'

Simone nearly died with fright at the sudden sound of Travis's voice. She jerked her head around and saw him leaning nonchalantly on the banister rail. 'I saw you from downstairs. Lurking about in the shadows—spying on people, Simone? Hardly your style, I would have thought!' He moved towards her and lifted the towelling belt at her waist. 'You should be dressed. Everyone's arrived.'

She wondered how he could talk to her so casually, so coolly. Didn't he understand that after everything he had said to her she detested the very sight of him?

'I'm...I'm not coming down—isn't that obvious?' Simone retorted, snatching the length of fabric from his fingers.

He released an impatient sigh and raised dark eyebrows. 'Because of what happened last night, I presume?'

Simone glared up into his face. 'Of course because of what happened last night!' she snapped wildly. 'Do you think I would want to spend a minute in your company after the things you said to me, after the way you deliberately set out to seduce me?

His mouth twisted into a smile. Damn him, he could actually smile about all that had happened! How could he do that, when her world was in ruins? 'Oh, come off it!' he drawled, shaking his head in disbelief. 'Deliberately set out to seduce? You don't honestly believe that!'

'You called me a tease!' she reminded him fiercely, changing tack, struggling not to explode with annoyance, because the angrier she became, the more he kept his infuriating cool.

'I was angry,' he replied evenly. 'You know that——'

'Oh, and that makes it all right, does it?' she hissed, her cheeks flushing red hot. 'Mr Steele was angry! So to hell with what he says or whom he hurts in the process!' She saw his jaw harden then. Dark brows drawing together in sudden sharp annoyance.

'You're determined to make an issue out of this, aren't you?' he said in a controlled undertone. 'God, Simone! Don't you have any idea of the things you were doing to me last night? I'm not super-human! I only have so much control, dammit! When I began to massage your back, *I* knew exactly where I wanted things to end—don't tell me you didn't too!' He pierced her with dark ebony eyes. 'Just like before, in the wood. You let me kiss you and touch you and then——'

'That's enough!' Simone rasped, covering her ears in despair. 'I don't want to hear any more!'

'Because it doesn't suit you to remember how it really was!' he retorted scathingly. 'Too easy to pretend that you had no part in what went on between us! Too easy to make me out as the villain of the piece! Well, it won't wash! For some reason you can't handle the fact that we both find each other attractive. That's your problem, not mine!' He glanced away and took a huge controlling breath. 'Stop acting like a frigid virgin, Simone! It doesn't suit you!' He spun back around and his eyes speared hers again, only this time there was a curious frown indented on his forehead. He gazed at her for a long moment before speaking. 'Are you a virgin?' he asked quietly. 'Is that what this is all about?'

Simone darted him a look of shock. A virgin! Oh, no! she thought. Oh, dear God!

It was as if the thought was a totally new one to Travis Steele. His ebony eyes covered her face with a searching glance. 'Are you?' he persisted when she didn't reply, only stared miserably into his face.

Simone gulped and felt the lurch of agony deep in the pit of her stomach. She closed her eyes for a brief moment and then opened them again, forcing herself to look at the man who had taken away her virginity five years ago and didn't have a clue that he had done so.

'How...how dare you ask me such a thing?' Her voice wobbled alarmingly.

'Is that a yes or a no?' he enquired impassively.

Simone took several ragged breaths and then she tilted her chin and speared him with a look of utter loathing. 'I'm no virgin,' she replied, shaking her head vehemently. 'Oh, no! I have been well and truly initiated in the art of sex—taught by a master of the subject! Why, don't look so disappointed, Travis!' she added with unrelenting coarseness. 'Were you hoping for a good catch? I know men think virgins are a particularly good scr——'

'That's enough!' he rasped, taking a step towards her, lancing her with a look that made her halt in her tracks. 'Don't you dare say another word!' He stared down at her for several heart-stopping seconds, intense distaste portrayed in his expression, and then he released a breath and when he spoke again she saw that he had regained control of his temper. 'Don't speak like that, Simone,' he muttered tightly. 'Never!'

He turned abruptly, every line of his masculine body portraying controlled anger, and began descending the staircase. 'Ten minutes!' he commanded. 'If you're not ready in that time, I'll come up and bring you down to dinner myself whether you're ready or not!'

She felt sick. Her legs hardly carried her back along the corridor to her bedroom. She sat on the bed and put her face in her hands. The nightmare was getting worse and she didn't know what she could do about it.

Leave, of course; that was the only way to escape this agony. And she would—in the end. But life was never that easy, never that straightforward. She had nowhere to go, no job to go to—easy as a gesture to pack her bags and flounce out of the house, but if she left now she would probably end up having to sleep in her car.

And of course there was Jake to consider. Her relationship with him was the only good thing to come out of this mess. Katy's cousin...

I don't want to go, a small inner voice whispered. Simone squeezed her eyes closed. She mustn't listen to her heart, she mustn't. It would be the surest way to destruction.

Travis thought nothing of her. He would use her and enjoy every minute of it and then he would discard her. And she would have to pick herself up from the floor all over again.

No. First thing tomorrow and she would start looking properly. She had her pride; it was still there, hanging by a thread maybe, but there all the same. She had to be strong.

But what about tonight? she asked herself. What are you going to do *now*? He didn't honestly expect her to go down and face him and his glamorous guests, behave as if everything was just perfect, did he?

Simone dragged herself up from the bed and paced the room almost frantically. Would he really put her through that?

Yes! Yes! her head told her. Haven't you worked it out even now? Why do you cling to the pathetic hope that inside, deep, deep inside, there's a man who possesses warmth and consideration? He will, without one shred of hesitancy, drag you all the way downstairs this evening, just to prove a sadistic point.

She didn't dare disobey him.

She got up and wrenched open the wardrobe door, bringing out the hanger with *his* dress on it, staring at the folds of gorgeous-coloured blue silk for a long time, fingering the fabric almost regretfully...

Ten minutes later and Simone took one last look at her reflection, twirling self-consciously in front of the full-length mirror. The halter neck plunged daringly, the curves of the full-length skirt skimmed her slim hips to just the right degree. It wasn't what she would have chosen for herself—not in a million years—but it did suit her.

Sophistication was clearly the order of the evening. The tall brunette had had on a gorgeous cream dress that just oozed money and good taste, so Simone had worked hard at fixing her silky honey-coloured strands into an elegant chignon, allowing a few wispy tendrils to escape around her hairline, to complete the desired effect.

With a trembling hand, she applied a last slick of deep rose lipstick, dabbed perfume at her wrists and her neck and then opened her bedroom door and descended the stairs with her heart pounding fit to burst.

It was almost eight-thirty. She could hear the muffled sound of voices coming from the drawing-room. Simone hesitated on the threshold and allowed her eyes to wander the room. Travis was over by the fireplace, in conversation with yet another glamorous guest.

Simone watched the two of them, her eyes lingering helplessly on his carved profile, the broad, rugged frame.

I love him, she thought. I love him so much.

It was like having a dagger thrust into her heart. The knowledge took her breath away, made her feel so incredibly sad. My girl, you sure are some masochist! she thought. To admit it *now*, *here*, in this room full of strangers . . .

He looked up and saw that she was there and his probing gaze just about destroyed her. He hates me, she thought. I've killed any chance there might have been. With a charming smile at his guests, he excused himself and crossed the room towards her.

Simone tilted her chin and tried to summon courage and determination and composure and a whole list of other resources she would need if she were to get through the evening, and found that she was found lacking in a whole load of vital departments.

'I was just about to come and find you! You've taken fifteen minutes.' He placed an arm around her shoulders and determinedly led her into the room.

'I'm here, aren't I?' Simone whispered fiercely, despising herself immediately, because the department that controlled physical awareness was already being tested and found wanting. 'What more do you want?'

'That you make an effort. Forget what's gone before and just enjoy the evening,' he replied quietly, handing her a fluted glass of bubbling champagne. His eyes shifted from her face to cover the length of her body in slow appraisal. 'The dress looks good, Simone.' It was almost as if he had forgotten he had company, she thought—or perhaps he didn't care that everyone in the room was eyeing them and silently speculating.

'Stop looking at me like that!' she murmured between gritted teeth. 'Everyone's watching!'

He tossed her a taunting, throw-away smile and then turned back towards the assembled guests. 'This is Simone, everyone. Jake's governess. Now as I know Mrs White is dancing about on tenterhooks because dinner was ready at least half an hour ago I think it would be best if we went on through into the dining-room.' Travis placed a guiding arm on Simone's bare back. 'I'll introduce you properly to everyone later.'

'Can't wait!' she murmured with a sarcastic smile.

She was placed at the far end of the table from Travis, which on one hand was a great relief and on the other was incredibly annoying. The beautiful brunette was at his right hand. Simone glanced up every now and then and found that the sight of the two of them in deep and often amusing conversation left her feeling incredibly miserable.

The food was extremely good. Mrs White had done Travis proud as usual. But the rest of the evening stretched interminably ahead, completely stifling any appetite that Simone might have had. There were twenty-four of them around the long mahogany dining-table, including Travis and herself.

The dinner seemed to last a lifetime. Simone was seated between a moustached man of about forty who, apart from commenting on the sad state of the world's economy, said very little, and a woman with silver hair, who seemed never to stop talking.

It got easier after three glasses of champagne. The pain inside dulled a little and Simone found she was able to say a few sentences to a rather good-looking young man opposite, who seemed, she noticed after a while, more interested in her cleavage than anything else.

Simone placed her dessert spoon down on her plate, defeated by the huge proportions Mrs White insisted on serving, and murmured yet another vague reply to the woman on her left.

At last dinner was dispensed with and they all moved back into the drawing-room for coffee and liqueurs.

Simone found herself next to the brunette. She had been told her name—what was it? Anna, a high-flying journalist on one of the 'better' women's magazines.

'Travis tells me you've not been here very long!' Red lips smiled engagingly. Simone placed her tiny coffee-cup carefully back on to its saucer and saw that the eyes didn't quite hold the same amount of warmth. She marshalled her thoughts. She had been thinking about something...*somebody* else, watching surreptitiously as he moved around the room. It was difficult dragging her mind back to party conversation, particularly as she had been practically dumb all evening.

'Just over a month,' Simone murmured.

'Travis told me that you've done absolute wonders for little Jake. He hopes to send him to school after the holidays, I believe. You'll be looking for another job then, I suppose?'

Simone looked into Anna's face and knew with complete certainty that she was, or had been at one time or another, Travis's lover. It was there, in her face, that mixture of forced casualness and desperation that told Simone she was well and truly snared.

Poor you, Simone thought. Poor us. Loving someone like Travis Steele...

'I'm going to start looking for a new place as soon as I can,' she replied quietly.

A look of relief crossed Anna's face and her eyes held slightly more warmth. 'You should have a word with Sally,' she murmured. 'See her? Over there in the green. I know she's looking for someone to help out with her brood. Come on, I'll introduce you.'

Simone found herself being led then by a suddenly determined Anna, over to a large group that unfortunately included Travis.

'Sally,' Anna interrupted brightly, 'you're in the market for nannies, aren't you? Didn't you say that your last one left with hardly any notice just before Christmas?'

'Well, actually I'm not really a nan——' Simone began.

'Simone here will be looking for a job soon. She's done such splendid work with Jake that he's back to school come the start of the new term. Isn't that right, Travis?' Anna purred, switching her gaze.

Travis's lips twisted into a smile. 'Well, well! I had no idea you were in the employment agency business,

Anna!' he drawled. 'How extremely helpful of you to take an interest in Simone's career prospects!'

Everyone laughed—all except Anna and Simone. Intimacy with the man, Simone mused, had, if nothing else, given them both a certain intuition into his moods—for some reason he was not particularly amused.

'I was simply trying to help,' Anna replied, a flush of embarrassment appearing high on each cheek. 'Simone told me she would be looking for a new post as soon as possible and I immediately thought of Sally...' Her voice trailed away as Travis's eyes raked her face.

How many women were there? Simone wondered. Who had been fooled by that man's seduction routine and lived to regret it or at least lived on in a kind of agonising limbo, as Anna surely did, just as she did, hoping for something that Travis would never, ever give?

'Well, Simone, if you are looking for another post, do say!' Sally said brightly, oblivious it seemed to the slight atmosphere that had befallen the group. She patted her prominent stomach, almost hidden beneath layers of bottle-green satin. 'My fourth child!' she announced proudly. 'I'm frightened to death that I shan't find anyone suitable and with little Katy on the way I want to be sure that everything's arranged in good time.'

Katy! Simone felt herself blanch at the sound of the name. 'You... you know that it's a girl?' she mumbled.

'Oh, yes! I decided forewarned was forearmed this time. With my other three I didn't want to know, but...'

It's silly to feel this way, Simone thought, as Sally babbled on; she's not talking about *my* Katy. Her mouth was dry. Simone licked her lips. Sickness churned in her stomach. I'll be all right, she told herself, fixing a smile, listening as Sally continued unmercifully with tales of her wonderful pregnancy, her hopes for her new daughter. I will!

But it was so hard, with Travis just a few feet from her, watching her with penetrating eyes; misery rose so swiftly, so easily. Simone took a deep controlling breath and found that it didn't help. Katy... Oh, it wasn't fair! She wanted her so badly, her own flesh and blood to love, to take care of...

'Simone? What's the matter?' Travis was beside her in an instant, placing a gentle hand on the bare skin at her shoulder. 'You don't look well.'

No! Don't touch me, she thought. Please! I can't handle it! Just leave me alone!

Simone pressed a hand to her mouth and tried not to feel ill, tried her hardest not to allow tears to well up into her eyes—she failed on both counts. Jerking herself free from Travis's supporting hands, she fled with mumbled apologies and streaming eyes from the drawing-room.

'Care to tell me what that was all about?' He hadn't bothered to knock. Simone raised her head from the pillow and saw that he lounged with infuriating assurance against the jamb of her by now open bedroom door.

'Go away!'

'You're crumpling that beautiful dress!' His voice was light. Simone wondered through her anguish why he wasn't angry with her for spoiling his precious evening.

'You think I give a damn about that?' Simone croaked, rubbing at her tear-streaked face.

'What *do* you give a damn about?' He was beside her

now, sitting on the edge of the bed. He raised his hand and fleetingly touched her face. 'Something, clearly.'

Simone jerked away, scrubbing at her face with a tissue, and dragged herself up into a sitting position. 'I...I had too much to drink.'

'You expect me to believe that's all it was?'

'I don't care what you believe!' Simone croaked. 'Just go! Go back downstairs and leave me alone! Your guests will be waiting for you.'

'I'm not leaving this bedroom until you tell me why you became so upset.'

Simone cast anxious eyes towards Travis's face. To say he looked determined would have been something of an understatement. He leant back against the head of the bed and folded his arms. 'I mean it, Simone,' he murmured. 'Tell me.'

'You honestly think I would tell you anything?' Her voice was deliberately scathing. She shifted her legs from under her and attempted to get up from the bed, but Travis was too quick for her, his fingers jerked to her arm.

'It had something to do with Sally. What did she say to upset you?' He looked fierce suddenly, and his fingers scorched into her skin.

'She...she didn't say anything to me!' Simone tried to prise his fingers away, but they were like bands of steel around her arm. 'You're hurting me! Let me go!' She began to cry, helpless tears of anguish and frustration, and with a muttered curse Travis released his hold and dragged her roughly into his arms.

Simone didn't have any energy left. To fight Travis, to fight the effect that being so near to him had on her, needed more resource than she possessed at that moment, would *ever* possess. He held her close and Simone closed her eyes and sobbed against the smooth wool of his jacket lapel.

'You're breaking my heart, Simone. Please, no more tears.' He lifted her away from him, wiping her tear-stained face with a pristine handkerchief. Breaking his heart? Did he mean it?

Simone sniffed and tried to hide her face from him, but he tipped her chin with one long tanned finger and forced her to look into his eyes. 'I think it's time to talk.'

What to say? Something, clearly. Some lie that would satisfy and get her out of this agonising situation. She hesitated, trembling beneath the dark, stunning gaze. A total blank. Nothing, except the awful heart-wrenching truth. Katy... Katy...

If he hadn't kissed her then, so gently, so sweetly, disarming her with all his powers, she might have held out. He placed the flat of his palm against her cheek and his lips moved over hers with slow, erotic hunger.

'Tell me,' he whispered, drawing his lips from hers, breathing the words over Simone's trembling mouth.

'I... I had a b-baby.'

There was a long silence. At last he spoke, just one word. 'Had?'

Simone gripped the bedcover and nodded faintly. She could barely see Travis's face through the veil of tears. 'What happened?' His head hadn't left her cheek. Simone could feel the warmth of his breath on her face.

She shook her head, her eyes narrowing, almost as if in physical pain. 'She died. P-please! I can't talk about it.' Her voice was barely a whisper. She felt drained. Just telling him this much was like baring her very soul.

'OK.' He stroked the wisps of hair back from her face and kissed her again and Simone felt the treacherous responses flaring up as his mouth covered hers with complete assurance. 'We'll talk later.'

He seemed reluctant to leave. His mouth moved over hers with slow hunger, again and again, and then with a sharp intake of breath and a smothered groan into the softness of her hair he dragged himself from her.

Simone watched as he strolled towards the door, noted the thoughtful expression as he turned and gave her one last look. 'I'll say you're not feeling well,' he murmured. 'Goodnight, Simone.'

She slept in the dress on top of the covers, waking at midnight at the roar of Ferraris leaving the courtyard. She sat up and rubbed wearily at her eyes, swollen and tender from so much crying, and then with the body of an old woman she went into the bathroom, stripped off the midnight silk and stepped beneath the shower. The hot, pounding spray made her feel marginally better, washing away the remains of her tears, soothing her reddened, blotchy face.

Simone wrapped a huge white bathsheet around her body and examined her reflection in the bathroom mirror. Travis knew that she had had a child—not his child, but she had revealed more than she wanted to and it frightened her like hell. For, sure as the sun rose in the sky each morning, she knew he would not be completely satisfied with her all-too-brief explanation. He had left her earlier because he had seen that she was too upset to talk and, of course, he'd had guests waiting, but later, perhaps as early as tomorrow, he would begin enquiring again.

Simone touched her lips and remembered the gentleness of his kiss. What was happening to her? How could she want him to hold her and touch her, when she knew that it meant nothing? When he kissed her and touched her, every particle of strength just melted away. When he was in the same room, all she could think of was him—where he was in relation to her.

I do love him, she thought. I really do.

Simone closed her eyes, clutching frantically at her head with both hands. What to do? How to stop this madness?

She picked up the midnight silk and draped it over her arms, carrying it through to the bedroom to hang back up in the wardrobe. At the sight of Travis, lounging casually on the window-seat, she stopped dead in her tracks.

I still underestimate him, Simone thought wildly. Why do I do that? She watched silently as Travis's stunning gaze travelled the length of her body, every nerve-end flaring under his potent male stare.

He's here because he wants me, Simone thought, and there's nothing I can do about it, because I want him too.

CHAPTER EIGHT

'HAVE they all left?' Simone whispered.

Travis moved towards her. 'All except one.'

'Oh?'

He lifted the dress from her trembling arms, dropped it to the floor. 'Yes, she's an enigma, this guest. Beautiful, intelligent, passionate...' He took Simone's hand in his. Lifted it to his mouth. Trailed a line of kisses along the delicate skin at her wrist, up towards the inner place at her elbow, pausing to hold Simone's gaze with stunning eyes. 'You see, she needs love and warmth—more than any woman I've ever known. She needs to be held in my arms, as I want to be held by her. But she fights and forces herself to be angry and cold and hard and somehow I find myself becoming that way too...'

More kisses. Up along her arm, towards her bare shoulders, sending waves of desire, shudders of need through the whole of Simone's aching body. 'I want you.' He breathed the words against the arched line of her neck, covered the delicate skin with feather-light kisses. 'No more fighting, Simone. No more pointless words...'

His mouth covered hers and Simone, quivering now with a need that was as fierce as his, wound her arms around his neck, parted her mouth, allowed his urgent tongue to probe the warm, moist interior.

I love you! I love you! she cried silently, as he lifted her in one swift movement and carried her over to the bed, placing her down with infinite care.

His hands travelled along the length of her body, over the mounds of her breasts, still hidden by the bathsheet, over the flat plane of her stomach, back again, this time to discard the offending garment with one swift, urgent tug. 'You're beautiful, so beautiful,' he breathed, running his hands along her burning skin, stroking and touching. His mouth fell to her breasts and Simone gasped with pleasure and felt the ache deep in the pit of her stomach as his tongue probed the darkened peaks.

She stretched up and fumbled frantically with the buttons of his shirt, her fingers sliding beneath the expensive linen, finding the mat of dark hair, stroking the expanse of tanned, muscled chest.

'Simone!' Travis's voice was ragged as he levered himself up and removed first his shirt and then the remainder of his clothing, his gleaming eyes never leaving her face, her body.

It was glorious, feeling the commanding, rugged length of him. Simone clawed his back dazedly as Travis's mouth began a journey of the most erotic intensity.

Five years of celibacy, five years of waiting for this... She wanted him now! Desperately needed to feel him inside her...

The first thrust of his possession was so beautifully intense that Simone gasped and moaned aloud. Travis stared down at her in the lamp-lit room and increased her pleasure again and again and again...

Afterwards she held on to him as if he were life itself, burying her face into his shoulder, linking her arms around his neck, pulling him close so that he shouldn't see her tears of emotion. I love you! I love you! The words wouldn't go away. Simone longed to whisper them out loud, longed to gaze into his wonderful face and tell him how she really felt.

She couldn't, of course. Ecstasy still lingered, but pain was following fast on its heels. She had succumbed again and even as Travis held her, kissed her, touched her, told her she was the most beautiful woman in the world, Simone felt the anguish deep inside, because morning would arrive, and with it reality.

Travis kissed Simone's neck and extracted himself from her grasp, to lie on his back, arms flung above his head. 'Mmm, that was good.' He expelled a sigh of pure satisfaction and turned his head towards Simone, who lay curled up in a ball beside him.

He looked so overwhelming, his deeply tanned, muscled body in stark contrast to the whiteness of the sheet at his waist. Simone allowed her eyes to wander over the flat, solid stomach, to the trail of dark hair that excited her tremendously even now.

Travis stretched out a hand and stroked Simone's cheek, his eyes slipping to the curves of her pale breasts, half hidden beneath her long golden hair. 'From the first moment,' he breathed, 'do you know what you've been doing to me?' His fingers stroked along the curve of her shoulder, down towards the valley between her breasts, a seductive smile turning the corners of his mouth as Simone shivered uncontrollably at his delicate touch.

He wanted her again. She could see it in his eyes, his mouth. His feather-light touch explored the pale skin of her body and persuaded her that she wanted him again too. Not that her treacherously aroused body needed much persuasion. They had just made deeply satisfying love, and yet every part of her ached to be held, to be possessed by him all over again. She kept so still, her breathing as shallow as she could make it. His hands continued their teasing exploration, on and on, expertly bringing her to a point of mindless sensuality, so that soon she was ready for his body all over again...

Simone awoke to find herself nestled in the curve of his arms. He was asleep, she knew instinctively. For a long while she listened to the rhythmic breathing, felt the fall and rise of his chest against her.

It was morning—early and still very dark. Simone closed her eyes and tried not to feel, tried not to think. It was impossible. Her thoughts swung from high to deep low. She knew that everything was a mess, that the night had only served to entangle her more deeply, that agony and pain would ensue as soon as the foolishness of her actions overcame the foolishness of her heart, but she also felt wonderful, lying next to him like this, sharing such beautiful intimacy...

Travis stirred against her and Simone automatically stiffened as his hand found and cupped her breast.

'Have you been awake long?' Travis murmured the words sleepily against the silky strands of hair. 'What time is it?'

Simone glanced towards the bedside clock. 'Just before seven,' she whispered.

Travis let out a sleepy groan. 'Mmm, far too early.' He kissed her shoulder. 'Go back to sleep, Simone.'

Who was he kidding? Sleep was the remotest of possibilities. Simone turned with difficulty and began to edge her way out of the bed.

'Where are you going?' Strong arms held her back, drew her close again, only this time she was facing Travis and that made everything ten times harder.

'I... I was just going——'

He found her mouth in the darkness and kissed away her words. Simone felt the immediate response of her own body as lips moved lazily, as his hands travelled the length of her body. 'Not just yet,' he murmured hungrily, moving so that his body was above Simone's. 'There's something I think we should do...'

Simone heard Travis's groan of sexual contentment as she herself gasped aloud and knew that there was no doubt this lovemaking session had been as perfect as all the rest. How many times? The thought passed fleetingly through her mind as she lay back breathing hard, her limbs sinking with delicious exhaustion into the mattress. Four? Five? Could she really have allowed Travis to make love to her so many times last night?

She turned her head and saw that Travis, propped up on one elbow, was staring down at her. The bedside lamp had been turned on, and she could see every part of him more clearly than she wanted to.

'You're blushing.' His voice was husky, teasing, full of laughter. He leant forward and kissed her full on the mouth, his tongue trailing sensuously along her lips. 'You look replete,' he murmured, 'totally and utterly fulfilled.' He kissed her some more, stroking strands of hair back from her face.

'I'm exhausted,' Simone admitted. She saw him smile and her heart turned over, twisting and hurting as it went.

'It was some night. You have the most wonderful body.' His mouth fell to her breast and immediately she felt the ache of response as his lips touched the darkened peak. 'Thank you.'

Simone felt the sting of tears. He was thanking her, as if... as if she had done him a favour, as if last night had been one of service of employee to employer. Was that how he saw it? Bad enough that she had been stupidly weak and succumbed. But that! Surely not! Surely...

The door opened slowly. Simone saw the crack of bright light out of the corner of her eye and hastily rearranged the bedcovers. Oh, no! Jake.

The door opened some more and then he marched into the room. Simone cast an anxious glance at Travis but saw no hint of awkwardness or embarrassment in his features. In fact he hardly moved a muscle when Jake approached the bed.

'Why are you in here, Travis?' Jake demanded, with his usual childlike bluntness. He glanced at Simone, who wished the whole bed would open up and swallow her, and then back to his uncle.

Travis adjusted the pillows so that he could sit up, and pulled Jake towards him, to perch on the edge of the bed. 'Miss Walker and I felt like a cuddle,' he explained lightly.

'Does that mean you like each other a lot now?' Jake asked hopefully, shifting so that he could sit more comfortably in the crook of Travis's arm.

Simone moved even lower under the bedclothes and shut her eyes in despair.

'Yes,' Travis replied firmly, 'it does. It means we like each other a lot.'

'But Miss Walker can't be your girlfriend, Travis, because she's my governess. I need her to teach me lots of things, don't I?'

'She can still do that, Jake. You don't need to worry, and besides, I don't think Miss Walker would like to be considered as my girlfriend anyway. Now why don't you go downstairs and see if you can help Mrs White with breakfast? Tell her I'm really hungry and I'll be wanting double everything!'

'OK!' Simone watched with relief as Jake jumped off the bed and dived for the door. 'Shall I ask Mrs White to bring you breakfast in bed?' he added.

Travis quirked one eyebrow and smiled wickedly down at Simone, who was still mulling over Travis's words—what had he meant about her not wanting to be his girlfriend? 'What do you think? Shall we have Mrs White bring up a tray?' Travis asked.

She gulped and shook her head and Travis's smile broadened. 'No, Jake, Miss Walker and I will come down in a few minutes.

'Well, that wasn't so bad, was it? Stop looking so petrified!'

Simone threw back the bedcovers and groped self-consciously for her gown. 'It was terrible!' she replied, without looking at Travis, thrusting impatient arms into the tangled robe. 'I felt like dying of embarrassment. What on earth will the poor child think?'

'Exactly what I told him. Which, in a much simplified form, is the truth. He's young; children of that age take everything at face value. Simone!' She turned finally at the insistent call of her name and met his persistent gaze. 'You make it sound as if we were doing something that was wrong, something that we should be ashamed of. Sex is natural between man and woman and what was shared last night was very, very good. You agree about that, don't you?'

'Yes—yes, I do.'

Travis's mouth curved into a heart-stopping smile. 'So why the worried expression? Nothing's changed, if that's what you're afraid of. Your status as Jake's governess isn't threatened in any way. We can carry on as normal.' He lay back against the headboard and stretched powerful arms above his head. 'Well, perhaps not quite so many arguments! I'm not sure I could cope with the mental exertion as well as the physical!'

Simone turned from him, struggling to find a voice that sounded reasonably bright, reasonably light. Her heart felt like lead, just listening to his flippant tone. 'Yes, yes, you're right, of course. Look, I'll just go and take a shower,' she murmured. 'See you downstairs at breakfast, OK?'

Jake was quite thrilled about something when Simone joined him and Travis at the table in the dining-room. He bounced up and down on his chair and chatted away cheerfully to a disapproving Mrs White, who removed lids from covered dishes with pursed lips. Simone didn't dare look at her. She didn't dare look at anyone. She had hardly been able to stand the sight of her own reflection in the mirror upstairs just a few moments ago.

'We're going to the pantomime!' Jake announced delightedly.

'We are?' Simone glanced towards Travis and raised enquiring eyebrows.

'I was given the tickets quite a while ago,' Travis explained. 'I thought it would be a treat for Jake. Will you come?'

Simone hesitated for just a fraction of a second and then nodded. It would at least fill some hours, give her a chance to decide what on earth she was going to do with this mess that was her life. 'Of course I'll come.' She turned and managed to smile at Jake, who tucked into a sausage and beamed with pleasure at the same time, so that a mixture of grease and tomato sauce dripped down his chin.

The well restored theatre, with its interior of rich red and gold, was overflowing when they entered. Jake's eyes darted everywhere as they took their seats in the box right near the stage. He hardly stopped talking, asking questions about everything and anything.

It was a good production. The scenery was just perfect. The dwarfs were funny. Snow White was beautiful with a strong, sweet voice and Jake enjoyed every minute.

He sat between them—Simone had made sure of that—but still Travis managed to touch her, with his arm flung casually along the back of the plushly upholstered seats, his fingers stroking her neck, massaging her shoulder, which tensed with every minute that passed, because while he touched her she couldn't think beyond how wonderful it had been last night, how good it was now to have him near her, wanting her still.

They came out just as it was getting dark. Travis took Jake's hand in his and wound his arm around Simone's waist.

In the bustling foyer people stared; she could feel their gazes burning into her back. Travis, despite his casual attire, still looked incredible, still made every woman's head turn. Simone knew she was noticed purely because of him.

Jake covered her silence in the Rolls on the way home, chattering non-stop until they reached home. He zoomed off to the kitchen almost before Travis had shut the front door to tell Mrs White everything.

'You know, I don't seem to have seen a great deal of you today,' Travis murmured, pulling Simone into his arms. His lips curved into a suggestive smile. 'Well, at least not as much of you as I would have liked. Do you know, halfway through the pantomime I very nearly gave way to the urge to take you in my arms?' He was kissing her with distraction, discarding her coat so that it fell to the floor, pressing her up against the double doors in the hall. 'Let's go to bed,' he suggested huskily. 'Jake will be with Mrs White for a long while yet.'

She wanted to—oh, how much! Her whole being ached with the need to feel safe and wanted in his arms. To be loved by him, if only in the physical sense, was all that mattered to her. When he touched and kissed and held her, as he was doing now, everything else, every other consideration, faded into oblivion.

Jake saved her—if only temporarily. Simone saw his small figure, watching with unembarrassed interest, and jerked free from Travis's embrace. She ran a shaky hand through her hair. 'T-Travis . . .' Her eyes shifted to where Jake stood.

'I want someone to read me a story.'

Travis moved his hand to rest lightly on Simone's waist, his lips curving into an amused smile at Jake's determined tone. 'Do you indeed?' He bent down and scooped Jake up into his arms. 'And who is going to do the reading?'

Jake stuck his thumb into his mouth—a sure sign that he was ready for bed—and considered thoughtfully. 'I don't mind. Both of you.'

Simone got out of it. She just couldn't face the prospect of a cosy little scene in Jake's bedroom. It would be too heart-wrenching for words. She didn't like disappointing Jake but she had to consider bigger things—like her sanity, for a start.

At the pantomime, she had pretended they were a real family, pretended that Travis felt more for her than just sexual desire, lust. It had been a wonderful two hours, kidding herself. Amazing what a buffer wild fantasy could be. But she couldn't fantasise forever. Reality had to emerge and take the lead at some point. Last night had been one long incredible fantasy trip and she was going to pay the price for that for a long time to come. Holding Travis close, loving him so desperately, imagining, as he possessed her over and over again, that he needed her, loved her, wanted her for more than her body.

'Can I come in?' Simone swung around from her position at the window with a jerk. Travis was in her bedroom anyway, whether she liked it or not. 'Jake's asleep,' he murmured, crossing the room towards her. 'The excitement of the pantomime has really tired him out.' He brought up a hand and stroked Simone's cheek. 'You're looking pretty washed-out yourself. Is everything OK?'

Simone turned her head and managed to side-step neatly to her left. Even a gentle word and a caress found her heart flipping wildly, caused an ache of desire deep in the pit of her stomach. She placed long slender fingers to her forehead and assumed a pained expression. 'I... I do feel a bit fragile,' she announced quietly. 'My head aches. I think I need an early night.'

'I'll run you a bath.' Travis walked purposefully towards the *en suite* bathroom. 'It will relax you.'

'No, don't trouble yourself!' Simone followed swiftly, pausing at the doorway to watch almost frantically as Travis turned on the elaborate gold taps. He poured in a generous portion of expensive oil from a height and turned to Simone with a smile.

'Simone, running a bath for you is no trouble at all. Come here,' he added huskily. 'I'll help you get undressed.'

'I... I can manage, Travis. Please, I...'

Her words faded into insignificance as Travis took hold of her hand and drew her towards the steaming bath. 'I want to help,' he replied. 'Stop resisting and just enjoy!'

His fingers fell to the button at the front of her dress and he began to unfasten with a touch that was far too deft. Simone hardly dared breathe as he slid the garment from her shoulders and allowed it to fall to the floor. She was wearing a coffee-coloured silk and lace teddy beneath and, after he had cast appreciative eyes over her choice of lingerie, his hands began to slip beneath the narrow straps at her shoulders.

'Travis, don't!' Simone placed a hand over his, stared at him with anguished blue eyes.

He raised one dark brow and his mouth curved into a disbelieving smile. 'Shy, Simone? Surely not. After last night? After all the beautiful things we did together?' She flushed, from her neck right up to the edges of her hairline. He traced his free hand along the line of her body, so that she shivered at his touch. 'I know what you need, Simone; trust me.'

Trust him? Oh, goodness! That was the last thing she should allow herself to do. She closed her eyes, partly in despair, partly because his touch was so wonderfully sensuous that it made her want to melt. 'Travis . . . you don't understand . . . I . . .'

His mouth easily silenced her halting sentence in a kiss that was warm and fierce with unmistakable passion. She trembled beneath his potent male touch, automatically released his hand, wound her arms around his neck as his lips moved hungrily over her own. On and on. The kiss lasted for so long that water began to lap over the edges of her bath, spilled on to the floor at their feet.

'We're going to drown, Simone.' His words were husky and slightly ragged as he leaned over and swiftly turned off the taps. He took a deep controlling breath and turned to her with a smile. 'Come on, time for your bath.'

There were no protests this time as Travis slipped the teddy from Simone's shoulders. But a bath wasn't what she wanted now; she wanted Travis to make love to her—now! This instant!

'Not yet, please!' She wound her arms around his neck, pressed her naked body against the rough denims and soft black cashmere, tugging shamefully at the jumper, pulling it free from the waistband of his jeans...

They made urgent, frantic love there and then. Simone pressed up against the huge gilt mirror that covered one wall of the bathroom, Travis using all his experience to achieve a climax for them both that was swift and incredibly satisfying.

They bathed together afterwards, and as Travis soaped her body with his large strong hands Simone played make-believe again and pretended everything was all right.

'Tell me about yourself.'

Simone stiffened, paused with the wine glass halfway to her lips. They had moved through to the bedroom. The warm glow of lamps filled the room; a tray of food rested on the bedside table. Simone forced her body to relax back against Travis's bare chest again. She took a sip of wine and shifted a little, pulled the sheet up some more so that it covered her naked breasts.

'You would be incredibly bored,' she replied lightly. 'There's nothing much to tell.'

Travis kissed the lobe of her ear. 'Let me be the judge of that. I want to know everything. I want to know what goes on in that beautiful head of yours. I want to know what makes you tick.'

'I'm a simple soul, Travis, honestly!' Simone tried to change the subject, began to talk about the pantomime, anything rather than herself.

It didn't work.

'Tell me about the baby.'

Simone closed her eyes, screwing up her forehead in despair. She ought to have been prepared. After all, he was the sort of man who didn't pull any punches. On the night of the dinner party she had seen in his eyes that he would want to know more... Should she tell him? Should she tell him *everything*? Part of her longed to, most of her. But that was because she was, at this very moment, living in fantasyland. In her dreams Travis couldn't live without her. In her dreams he wanted her for more than just sexual satisfaction. In her dreams he would be understanding, and distraught. He would hold her and somehow make everything all right... Katy! Katy! The name shrieked inside her head. Travis's daughter... What was she *doing*?

'Travis, I don't particularly want to talk about it. Years have passed. It's history. I had a baby and she didn't live more than a few hours. End of story.' Simone gave a forced half-laugh. 'I don't know why I got so uptight about it the other evening. I really haven't thought about that part of my life in a long, long time.'

'And the father?'

She spilled a drop of wine on to the sheet and mopped hastily. 'Oh, I... I...' She swallowed and tried to think. 'The father...I...I never knew...' Simone's voice trailed away. She hadn't the first idea of what to say.

'You mean you didn't know who the father was?'

'N-no.'

'I see.' His tone was disapproving. Simone wondered why it should be so and then realised with a wave of shock that he had taken her answer the wrong way. He thought she had slept around, that there was more than one lover to choose from...

'Are you on the Pill, Simone?'

Her heart sank at the sudden bluntness of his question, the slight change in his voice. What to do? Put him right? Explain that it wasn't the way he thought? That there had just been one man, one unforgettable experience? That the man she had fallen for then had lost none of his powers, none of his ability to turn her life inside out, upside-down? Simone hesitated a moment.

'You're aware that in the bathroom I didn't——?'

She nodded her head and replied in a subdued voice. 'Yes, it's all right. I am on the Pill.' What was she saying? She wasn't! Never had been! But she didn't want him to know that now, didn't think she could face his anxiety about an unwanted baby. If she was pregnant... The thought struck her for the first time. To carry his child again, that would be something. She had lost Katy, she would never have his love, but she could have a part of him that way. Instinctively her hand slid to her stomach. Was it possible she was pregnant by him?

'What are you thinking?'

'N-nothing.'

'Simone, why do you insist on shutting me out? One minute I feel as if I'm beginning to get close to you and the next——'

Simone threw back the bedclothes suddenly and got out, dragging a discarded robe around her quivering body. 'Where are you going?'

'I feel like some air,' she replied, thrusting impatient feet into her mules. 'To clear my head.'

'Now?' Travis raised one dark brow in query as Simone made for the bedroom door. 'You're not going to actually go outside, are you?'

Simone tilted her chin defiantly. 'I am,' she replied firmly. 'Why shouldn't I?'

'Because it's below freezing out, you're not dressed and because it's late and because I——'

'Fancied some more sex?' Simone finished bluntly, clasping the door-handle so tightly that her knuckles whitened.

Travis looked at her without speaking for a long moment, puzzlement written clearly in every line of his furrowed brow. When he spoke, his voice was hard and cold. 'There seems suddenly to be a problem. Care to tell me what it is?'

She glanced from his face and stared at the closed door, her back towards him. It took quite a while to form the words, but eventually she managed it. 'I've made a mistake,' she murmured shakily, repeating the sentence again, but more clearly the second time, almost as if convincing herself. 'I should never have let things happen like this.'

'You regret our making love?' His tone held harshness and incredulity too.

Simone nodded at the door, not daring to turn and see the expression on Travis's face. 'Yes,' she whispered.

'You dare to stand there and say that?' he barked. 'For goodness' sake, turn around! Have the decency to look at me!'

What expression had she expected to see on that incredibly handsome face? Anger, of course. Shock? Regret? Any number of emotions that would give clues to how he really felt. None was evident. Controlled anger, maybe, but that was about all. Which shows, Simone reminded herself, just how little you mean to him. His pride's been hurt, of course. No man, least of all Travis Steele, likes to be told his lovemaking, particularly when it is of such a high standard, has been one big mistake.

'I think it would be better if I looked for another post straight away,' Simone managed shakily. 'I'm a professional. I should never have allowed my personal life to get mixed up——'

'To hell with that!' Travis cut in savagely. 'I couldn't give a hoot for your profession, or your ethics!'

'Oh, I know you couldn't!' Simone retorted with sudden, angry fire. 'As long as you're having a good day! As long as your incredible sexual appetite is being pandered to! Well, thanks for a good time, but I have other things to consider.' She wrenched frantically at the door. 'It's taken me a long time to build my life back up again and I won't let you destroy it, Travis. I won't let you destroy *me*!' Her lip trembled and she heaved a controlling breath. 'Heaven knows I should have learnt my lesson by now, but obviously I haven't! Obviously where you're concerned I'm a very slow learner.' She pierced him with a determined look. 'I'm going to leave at the end of the week.'

CHAPTER NINE

'YOU think I'd let you go that easily?'

Simone had underestimated his speed. Travis was at the door before she could open it.

'I...I don't see you have much choice.' Her voice wobbled alarmingly. 'If...if I want to leave I will. There won't be a thing you can do about it.'

'And what do you propose to live on?' Travis enquired. 'Presumably you would need to find another post pretty swiftly. Any future employer would almost certainly come to me for references.'

'You wouldn't dare!'

'Oh, I would, Simone. Make no mistake about that! I don't want you to leave. I like the way we are together. When we're in bed there's a spark, something special, something that I've not encountered since...' He shrugged his shoulders and his lips twitched into an infuriating smile. 'Well, let's just say in quite a while.'

No mention of love—not that she had ever expected any, she reminded herself swiftly. But not even affection, an acknowledgement that he found her at least likeable as a person. Good in bed together—that was all that mattered to him. Nothing had changed—perhaps the frequency with which he went after bedmates, but in essence all Travis Steele was interested in was physical satisfaction.

She wanted to cry. To sob long and hard. She had brought all this pain on herself, of course—she should have handed in her resignation straight after that first moment of recognition—but it didn't make the anguish any less hard to bear.

'I don't want you to go.' He pressed Simone back against the door and kissed her mouth very gently, almost sweetly, so that she was shocked instantly into stillness, his tongue trailing sensuously along her lips. He was naked against her and Simone could feel every inch of his taut, powerful frame, knew that with just a touch of his hand he could persuade her, in that moment, to anything. 'Don't fight it, Simone,' he whispered huskily, releasing her mouth to breathe the words against her neck. 'Come back to bed. Let me remind you how very good we are together.'

She nearly succumbed, despising herself all the while for even considering it, for trembling, as she allowed his hands to trace a delicate path over her body. 'No!' In the dying embers of self-will, she placed her hands up against his sculpted chest and pushed, twisting her mouth away, tensing her body into a rigid form. 'No, I won't! I can't! You must understand!'

'How can I understand, when you choose not to tell me?' Travis demanded grimly. 'I want to know you—who you are, how you feel. Why do you keep shutting me out like this?'

'Please! I can't take any more!' She knew she sounded desperate, like a woman on the verge of hysteria.

Travis stepped back, released her, watching with burning eyes as Simone rearranged her robe. 'So,' he murmured with menacing softness, 'you really are determined to ruin everything. Why? What is it? Can't you handle happiness?'

'Happiness?' Simone spat the word back in his face. 'You think I could be happy, living here like this? Being used by you, simply because we're good in bed together?'

She shook her head, dared a look at Travis's expression and immediately wished she hadn't, because frightening, dark anger was evident in every inch of his face.

'That's how you see it?' His voice was as hard as steel.

'Of course that's how I see it! That's how it is!' Simone almost yelled. 'I'm not a fool, so don't you dare start treating me as one! I was a fool before and look where that got me!' She was shaking so much that she thought she was going to fall over. She leant back against the closed door and tried to calm herself down, tried to prevent all composure from deserting her completely.

'You slept around—what do you expect?'

Simone stared in amazement and then her hand jerked up and she hit him across one tanned cheek with every ounce of her force. 'How dare you?' she croaked. 'How dare you say that to me?'

He didn't move—not one inch. 'I'm sorry. I shouldn't have——'

'No! But you did, didn't you? You just couldn't help yourself!'

'Simone, look at us! Look at what we're doing, what we're saying to each other. This doesn't make any sense——'

'I shouldn't have slept with you,' Simone repeated desperately. 'Please just accept that and let me go.'

Travis's dark gaze raked her body. 'If you leave before the week is up, you won't see a penny of your wages,' he snarled softly. White teeth flashed predatorily against his tanned skin. 'I can be quite alarmingly ruthless on occasions, Simone. When I've decided I want something I get it—one way or another.'

'Miss Walker, I'd like a word with you in my study. Mrs White, would you look after Jake for a while this morning, please? He's a bit upset. Perhaps a spot of baking to take his mind off things.'

Simone stared at the sharply closed kitchen door when Travis had gone and then cast a glance at Mrs White and Minnie, who had halted in their conversation and were looking at Simone with an expression that told her they knew exactly what was going on and that all the turmoil now was undoubtedly due to her.

Three days of agony. That was what it had been. Stupidly, Simone had somehow imagined it would get easier. Distancing herself from him, hardly speaking, never touching, never even thinking... She had been searching like mad for a new job, scouring the papers, the professional journals, racking her brains for somewhere, some way to earn her living when she left at the end of the week. Just four days to go and her desperation was increasing. She had even, in a moment of despair this morning, considered giving Sally a ring, offering herself as nanny to her brood, but the thought had been too awful to contemplate. Travis was a friend and there would be baby Katy...

No. To get right away, that was the only solution.

Simone picked up her cereal bowl and coffee-mug from the kitchen table and walked across to the dishwasher.

'Here, I'll take those,' Mrs White said, removing the dishes from Simone's hands. 'You get along and speak to Mr Steele. He sounded mighty annoyed about something.'

'And we wouldn't want that, would we?' Simone murmured sarcastically, suddenly irritated by the elderly woman's tone. They blame me, she thought, for the atmosphere that's shrouded this house over the last three days. They think it's all my fault. After all, wonderful Travis Steele couldn't possibly be to blame, could he?

'Why is Jake upset?' Simone asked, as she entered Travis's study and closed the door behind her. 'I saw him earlier this morning and he seemed quite all——'

Travis was on the phone. Simone had knocked and then walked straight in. She hesitated as he swivelled round and was about to retreat when he raised his hand, making it plain that she should stay.

'Yes, Phil. She's here with me now. Would you like a word?' Travis lowered the receiver from his ear and placed a hand across the mouthpiece. 'This is a business colleague,' Travis informed her in completely neutral tones. 'He's got three children—two at boarding-school. He wants a governess for the youngest. I told him you were looking for another post. Speak to him nicely and it's practically settled.' He held out the receiver. 'And there's no need to look like that, Simone. He lives up in Yorkshire, that's plenty enough miles from here, and I've visited his home perhaps twice in ten years of acquaintance. So the likelihood of our meeting ever again is practically non-existent.'

With a grimace that didn't completely cover her look of complete dejection at the scathing, hardened tones in Travis's voice, she took the phone and found herself conversing pleasantly with a well-spoken man. It happened so quickly. In a matter of moments Simone found herself arranging a time and a date for an interview, for a job she hadn't been aware of two minutes ago and wasn't sure that she even wanted.

'You'll like them.'

Simone turned from gazing out of the window at the view she had come to love and tried to assemble her thoughts into an orderly procession. It was hard keeping a tight rein on them all of the time. They skitted about so dreadfully, so treacherously. She swallowed, watching as Travis signed some letters, and felt a sickness settle in her stomach at the thought of leaving him. 'Who?'

'The Carter family.' He spoke without looking up, his voice cool and detached. 'Phil's solid and dependable and Gina, his wife, is quite a scatterbrain and full of fun. You'll get on well together, I should imagine.'

Was he doing this deliberately? she wondered, hugging her arms around her body. Making her feel a hundred times worse with this sudden change in his attitude? Three days ago he had been so determined to have her stay; now it sounded as if he didn't much care one way or another.

'When are you seeing him?'

Simone tried to force resolution into her voice and failed miserably. 'Tomorrow.'

'So why so glum?' Travis enquired in a clipped voice. 'This is what you wanted, isn't it?'

She turned to look at him again, her heart leaping somersaults as she took in every last scrap of his physical appearance. He was dressed casually this morning: faded denims topped with a chunky rust pullover, the sleeves pushed up to reveal strong forearms covered in thick black hair. She watched his hands holding the gold fountain-pen, moving swiftly from letter to letter, and tried not to remember how wonderfully they had touched her, how intimately...

'I thought you didn't want me to leave.' Her voice was quiet, so quiet that Travis didn't catch what she said.

'Pardon?' He raised his head at last and looked at her and she felt a flush of awareness as his eyes bored into her face.

'I...I just wondered why you were bothering to help me find a job,' Simone murmured faintly.

'I told Jake this morning that you were leaving.'

Simone's eyes widened. 'You did *what*? But——'

'And I think it's best now that you go sooner rather than later,' Travis continued with determined quiet, stifling Simone's angry response with clipped, controlled syllables. 'You've had little success finding somewhere else, haven't you? I knew Phil had been looking for a while for someone suitable——'

'But... but you had no right to tell Jake I was going!' Simone retorted angrily. 'I wanted to break it to him gently, to talk to him properly about my decision...' Tears were welling up in her eyes. Simone spun back towards the window, frantically trying to compose herself sufficiently to carry on. 'What... what did you say?' she asked. 'I suppose you were blunt and hard and——'

'I simply gave it to him straight.'

'Exactly!' Simone snapped. 'Without any thought to his feelings.'

'So when were you proposing to inform him?' Travis rasped with sudden anger. 'Today, tomorrow, or just as you got in the car with your suitcase? It's been three days since you informed me you were leaving. There must have been any number of occasions when you could have told Jake that you were going. Do you know what he said to me this morning?' he added with sudden quiet.

'I was going to tell him today,' Simone replied croakily.

'Do you know what he said to me this morning?' Travis repeated insistently.

Simone glanced nervously across at him, aware of the undertone of controlled anger in his voice. 'No,' she breathed. 'What did he say?'

'Jake asked me when we were going to get married. He wanted to know if you were going to have a baby. He particularly asked for a brother, even got as far as suggesting some names.' Travis's smile didn't hold warmth. Simone watched the harsh curve of his lips, the almost bleak look in his eyes and wondered how much more anguish she could take. 'So,' Travis continued unmercifully, 'I thought it best to put him in the picture right away. You can imagine his response.'

Simone shook her head inadequately. 'I...I didn't want it to be like this...' I don't want to go, she thought. I don't! 'When he's back at the village school, he'll feel better. I'll just be a vague memory...he'll forget I ever existed.'

'You think so?'

'Yes.'

He threw down his fountain-pen in a violent gesture and stood up, leaning both hands on the desk. 'You just haven't a clue, have you, Simone? Not the faintest idea! I warned you about allowing Jake to become too attached. I made it clear that it was a dangerous, futile and in the end downright cruel exercise! Jake is especially vulnerable emotionally. You knew that and yet you continued to allow him to get close!'

'I couldn't help it!' She spun away, her voice raw with emotion, her eyes filled with tears.

'Just as you couldn't help allowing me to make love to you, I suppose?' His voice was scathing. Simone felt the tightness in her throat increase as his derisive tones continued. 'You don't look beyond the moment, do you, Simone? You don't stop and consider where things are going to lead——'

Simone spun round violently. 'I'm not a machine!' she retorted hoarsely. 'I'm a woman! I can't switch my feelings on and off. I can't be someone, something I'm not! Jake and I...' She shook her head, trying to explain something that was just too simple to put into words. 'There was an instant rapport. I didn't go about trying to foster it—it just happened.'

'And with me?' His eyes held hers. They were blacker than she had ever known them, deeply intense, although there was no indication of expression anywhere else in his face. Just his eyes, looking straight at her, watching for every tiny response.

Simone released a taut breath. 'You... you know very well how it was,' she replied shakily, struggling to hang on to her composure.

'Tell me!' Travis instructed with sudden harshness. 'I'm curious as to how you see our relationship.'

'Relationship?' Simone gave a derisive laugh. 'That's a joke! I hardly think our two sexual encounters qualify for the grand title of relationship—not in any meaningful sense anyway.' Simone stung Travis with a look of sheer contempt. 'You set out to seduce me from almost the very first moment, didn't you? Didn't you?' Simone repeated insistently, almost wildly, when Travis made no move to answer.

'Yes.'

She managed a smile. It practically cracked her face, but she succeeded somehow to convey a picture of, if not casual indifference, at least calm acknowledgement. 'Well,' she croaked, 'at least you're being honest! You used me—and I used you. Physical satisfaction. You were right, Travis, it was good. But I made a mistake. I'm a professional. To live here, teaching Jake and... No!' She shook her head vehemently, her eyes flashing wildly, as Travis made as if to come around the desk towards her. 'Don't...don't come near me. There's nothing more I have to say to you. Where's Jake now?' she added in subdued tones, a frown creasing her forehead. 'I must talk to him myself.'

Travis looked at her for a moment longer and then returned his attention to the paperwork on his desk. 'He'll be in the kitchen. But I don't think it will be a good idea to speak to him for a while yet. You're not his favourite person at the moment, as you can imagine.'

Perhaps it was for the best, Simone thought as she fled from Travis's study. If Jake hated her, then parting wouldn't be so hard for him. If only the lack of feeling she displayed so admirably on the surface for Travis could be forced somehow to take over on the inside, could consume the overwhelming love that hurt her so much. If she hated him, or if there was just the indifference which she had so clearly witnessed on his face just now, she wouldn't be feeling as if her life was coming to a premature end. She wouldn't be feeling so desperately lonely and unloved.

'Jake, please let me speak to you.'

He was playing outside, bouncing a bright orange ball up and down on the paving outside the french windows that led to the enclosed rear garden. Simone placed a fleeting hand on the baseball cap that was far too large for him, but a gift from Travis and therefore treasured immensely, and found it shrugged away.

'Can't we be friends still?' Simone asked, desperation creeping into her voice. 'I don't want to leave having you think badly of me.'

'I don't care if you go now anyway,' Jake informed her, sticking out his bottom lip in defiance. 'Travis told me we're going to get someone else to look after me. And this time if Travis has to go away he's taking me with him!'

Simone watched Jake scuff his boot along the paving slab and felt a lump rise in her throat. 'Well, that will be nice,' she managed brightly. 'It sounds as if you're going to be very, very busy. You'll go to lots of exciting places, be able to see lots of exciting things, won't you? And now that you're such a big boy and are going to school you won't need a silly teacher like me at home anyway, will you? Think of all the new friends you're going to make.' Simone closed her mouth abruptly, realising that she had begun to prattle. She wanted Jake to be happy and she was trying too hard. 'I'm... I'm going to miss you very much Jake,' she began, struggling to form the things she wanted to say into a coherent sentence. 'I've... I've never taught such a clever, friendly boy before...' She gulped and pressed her lips together, struggling against the tears. 'And you must understand that I'm not leaving because I don't like you any more, or because I want to go somewhere else because I think it's going to be better. It's just... well... I was never meant to stay here very long. I only came in the first place to help you until you felt more like your old self.'

'Do you *have* to go, Miss Walker?' Jake had turned, was looking up at Simone with huge watery dark eyes. The corners of his mouth were drooping down in a picture of complete misery that mirrored Simone's own expression completely.

Words were impossible. She just nodded, managed a regretful half-smile and then turned and fled back into the house.

'I should be back around lunchtime tomorrow.' Simone shivered as she stood on the front steps and told herself it was because of the sharp, bitter north wind—not because Travis was standing in the doorway, making everything ten times, no, a hundred times more difficult by coming out to see her off.

'You're sure you want to go in that thing?' His eyes shifted from her face to throw a glance at the yellow Mini parked behind. 'Why don't you catch a train? Charles could drive you to the station.'

'I'm fine—thank you.' Simone delved in her bag for her car keys.

'You've got the directions?'

She nodded, trying not to mind about the stiffness that there was between them, the cold, distant formality. 'Yes.'

'OK. See you some time tomorrow.' He turned then without a backward glance and went back into the house.

She had been invited by the Carter family to stay the night. As long as she had no other plans, it would give her, Phil had suggested on the phone, a good chance to get to know them, to get a feel of the household.

It was pretty plain, Simone thought as she negotiated the Mini on to the motorway, that she had the post if she wanted it. Travis had obviously put an excellent word in for her—but then he would have done. He wanted rid of her as soon as possible.

She took her time getting there, deliberately driving at a slower speed, working hard at fostering a relaxed attitude, so that she shouldn't get to York in a frazzled state of mind. There was a tight ball of anguish inside her, a knot of misery that she knew would never go away. She had lost Katy, lost Travis. No, that wasn't right. How could she have lost something she'd never possessed? Travis didn't love her, never had, never would, but she was determined to appear serene and calm, capable and professional on the surface. She was determined to make the best of the situation and accept this as a way out.

It was quite a drive, motorways had never been Simone's favourite method of getting from A to B, and she was more than a little relieved when she pulled off at the correct exit and progressed into the beautiful Yorkshire countryside.

She was waiting at a set of traffic-lights, wondering if she had taken the right turn, drumming fingers idly on the steering-wheel in time to the frenetic beat on the radio, when out of the corner of her eye she saw a small hand clutching on to the back of the passenger-seat beside her. A wave of absolute astonishment flooded through every part of Simone's body. She turned sharply and watched as Jake emerged bleary-eyed from beneath the tartan blanket on the floor behind her.

'Jake! What on earth——?'

The lights had changed, probably some time ago, if the amount of horn blaring was anything to go by. Simone jerked her head round, thrust the car into gear, stalled, tried again and finally shot off into the traffic ahead. 'Jake, what are you doing here?' It was an obvious first line. Simone had a very good idea why Jake had stowed himself away, but she couldn't, at that moment in time, think of anything else to say.

'I wanted to see where you were going. I fell asleep.' He rubbed small hands over his face. 'Are we nearly there? I'm very hungry. I had to miss my breakfast so that I could hide in your car.'

'Jake, you know you shouldn't have done this. Travis will be very worried about you.' Simone glanced at her wristwatch. It had been over four hours since she had left. Travis would be more than worried, he would be frantic.

'It's all right, Miss Walker,' Jake informed her seriously. 'I didn't come without leaving a note. I put it in my special place for messages—in the box on my toy shelf.'

'But Jake,' Simone explained as calmly as she could, while scanning the unfamiliar roads for a telephone box, 'Travis doesn't know about your special place, does he? I remember you only told me it was a secret place, just for you and your toys. How will he know where to look?'

The thought obviously hadn't occurred to young Jake. His face began to crumple, his bottom lip trembled and in the next moment he was wailing out loud.

Simone pulled the Mini over to the side of a deserted road as quickly as she could and brought him into the front seat to sit on her lap. 'It's all right, sweetheart. I'll sort it out,' Simone murmured soothingly as he sobbed into her shoulder. 'We'll find a telephone and phone Travis. He won't be angry once he knows you're safe.'

The first time the line was engaged. Ten minutes later and Simone still couldn't get through, so she suggested going to a small village teashop, which cheered Jake up enormously.

She looked at her road map, while Jake tucked into a gooey cream cake, and calculated that she had just under an hour's driving before she got to her destination. So what should she do? Carry on, or turn back straight away and take Jake home?

After two cups of tea and a long, hard think, Simone decided to return. She couldn't face taking Jake to the Carters' house, having to wait while Travis came for him, seeing the look on the poor child's face as he left her all over again. No, she would take him back herself.

The drive wasn't something she particularly relished, not so soon anyway, so she bought a few things for a picnic and a bright multi-coloured football and took Jake to a small picturesque park that had a lake and some swings and slides.

'It's going to be all right—don't look so worried. I think the receiver's been left off accidentally,' Simone explained to an anxious-looking Jake. She had been trying Travis's number almost continually and had still had no luck. 'I phoned the operator and she said it's not out of order. Best thing is to get back as soon as possible. Now jump into the car and we'll play some of these story cassettes that I've bought for you on the way home.'

She realised about five miles down the motorway that she hadn't thought to phone the Carter household. In her preoccupation with letting Travis know Jake was safe it had completely slipped her mind. And, she thought, worriedly, Travis would be sure to contact them at some stage. He would be even more concerned to find out that she hadn't arrived on time. 'Damn!' Simone muttered out loud, so that Jake looked across and asked her what the matter was. 'I've just forgotten to do something, Jake,' she murmured, concentrating hard on overtaking an irritatingly slow vehicle ahead. 'It will be all right.'

But it wasn't all right. Not at all. When she finally swung the Mini into the courtyard, there was a police car parked in front of the house and Travis was outside in the late afternoon gloom, talking to a policeman.

She would never forget the expression on his face when he saw the Mini, herself, Jake. Grim described his expression exactly, unflinching eyes watching as she brought the car to a halt.

Simone stared at him through the windscreen and felt a surge of love, uncontrollably intense, race through her.

He had been worried sick, she could tell, even though not a flicker of emotion showed itself on his face.

Travis said something to the policeman, who smiled and got back into his car and then Jake was out of the Mini and bounding towards his uncle. Simone looked on, watching with tears in her eyes as the two hugged, as Travis picked up his nephew and spoke to him seriously.

'Why the hell didn't you let me know he was with you?'

Jake had run on into the house, unconcerned now he had said his apologies, promised never to do such a thing again.

Simone shut the door of her Mini with a bang, annoyed with herself as much as anything for foolishly half expecting the same sort of welcome as Jake. 'Don't you think I tried?' she retorted angrily, running a weary hand across the ache in her forehead, walking round to the small boot to retrieve her overnight bag.

'Not hard enough, no! What is it? Don't they have telephones up north?' Travis enquired sarcastically. 'Too much trouble to simply pick up the receiver and put me out of my misery?'

Simone stared into his taut face, listened to the thudding of her own heart. How can he do this to me? she thought. Can't he see how I feel? How much I need him? 'The line was engaged,' she informed him coolly. 'I tried many, many times. Ask Jake if you don't believe me!'

'Do you know the sort of agony I've been through today,' Travis rasped, 'when Jake couldn't be found? I imagined all sorts—from injury to kidnap to murder. And then when I phoned Phil Carter and found you hadn't turned up on time...! I had half suspected Jake might be with you at first, but when I had no word . . .!' He shook his head angrily. 'Why on earth did you take so long to come back? What was it? A way of punishing me for enticing you into my bed—letting me go through hell imagining both you and Jake were dead?'

Simone stared dazedly up into his face, her clear blue eyes large with disbelief. How could he think that of her? He believed that she would be so cruel? The thought made her feel sick. She shook her head bleakly and wondered how she could love him so much when it was clear that he disliked her so intensely. 'How . . . how can you believe I would do such a thing?' Her voice was quiet, full of despair and misery as she stared into the ebony eyes. 'How could you? Do I really rate so low as a person in your eyes?'

'Simone . . .' Travis ran strong hands through his hair and the expression on his face suddenly mirrored her own. 'Simone, I'm sorry! I didn't mean any of that——'

'But you said it! And words can't be retrieved once they're spoken!'

'Simone, can't you understand what I've been going through?' Travis's voice was harsh, his eyes bleak. 'I lost my sister and brother-in-law in a motorway pile-up and the longer time went on after I had phoned Phil Carter and found out you hadn't reached him, the more the memory of their crash penetrated my mind. I had a pretty good idea he would be with you and I expected you to phone—when you didn't——'

'Don't!' Simone twisted her head away and tried to cover the flood of tears that was spilling on to her cheeks. It had been a long, hard, frustrating day. She knew exactly how Travis had felt, understood his anxiety when she hadn't called, but the fact was he had still talked to her so coldly, so cruelly... 'Just let me get into the house. I'm fed up, worn out and absolutely sick and tired of the way you tr-treat me!' Her voice didn't stay as steady as she wanted it to. She turned and pushed past him and ran on shaking legs in through the large oak front door.

CHAPTER TEN

'YOU are not going anywhere until we get this straight, until I know you understand!' Travis caught Simone, holding her around the waist with one arm. 'Look, what else can I say except I'm sorry? Don't storm upstairs. I don't want us to fight all over again. Will you please just forget everything I said out here? I've been worried sick. The thought that I might have lost both you and Jake...' He pulled her back against his broad chest and Simone felt the warmth of his breath against her cheek. 'You must understand... Jake...well, Jake, he means everything to me.'

She had dreamed in that split-second of hesitation, foolishly harbouring hope in her heart, pathetically holding her breath, waiting for the words, some indication that *she* actually meant something to him. She closed her eyes. 'I know he does,' she breathed.

'Do you understand how I felt, why I let rip without thinking?'

She took a deep breath. 'Yes, I...I understand. Please,' she added shakily. 'Will you let me go now? I'm...I'm very tired.'

'What about the Carters?' Travis murmured softly. 'Are you going to phone, or do you want me to do it?'

She couldn't think straight. Travis hadn't released her. His arm was still around her waist, the strength of his fingers pressing her firmly against his body. All day she had longed to be back in his arms, longed to feel safe and warm, longed to hear his voice telling her she meant something to him. 'Shall I tell Phil you've changed your mind?' he added, when she didn't reply.

There was silence—or at least there would have been if Simone's heart hadn't been pounding fit to burst. Was he asking her to stay? Was that what he was saying? She hesitated, tried to read something more into his words.

'Come upstairs with me,' he breathed against her hair. 'Let me make everything right between us.' His mouth grazed her cheek, and she shuddered as his hand stroked down the length of her thigh. 'Let me touch you and hold you. Let me show you how much I want you.'

His words lanced through her heart. Every inch of his body exuded passion, deep and intense. He wanted her—but he didn't love her. He needed her body for the satisfaction and release of sexual intercourse, but he didn't need her mind, her soul, her love... How long had it been? Three, almost four days, she calculated swiftly; quite a long wait, she supposed, for someone as sexually active as Travis Steele.

'Please, Travis, stop this!' She heard herself say the words, listened to the lack of conviction in her voice, felt the searing exquisite sensation of physical desire and his hands moved to cup her breast, as his mouth found her lips and easily penetrated the moist interior. She closed her eyes and allowed endless seconds to pass before finally finding the strength of mind and body to pull free. 'You know I can't stay here, Travis!' she cried wildly. 'N-nothing's changed between us.'

She placed a foot on the stairs, aware that she was shaking like a leaf, feeling as if she had been dragged through an emotional hedge backwards. 'I'll phone Mr Carter and... and make my apologies,' she added in a stumbling voice. 'He'll understand. Perhaps I'll be able to go up tomorrow.'

'If that's what you want.' His voice was neutral, polite and bordering on the formal once again.

It's not what I want! Simone yelled silently, turning away from him, climbing each stair, which felt like a mountain. Can't you see that? Can't you understand how much I need you to *love* me?

If only I had someone to confide in, Simone thought early next morning. Keeping everything locked up inside like this, going over and over all that has happened, all that I feel . . . She was taking a bath, mounds of bubbles, lots of hot water, pampering herself with any amount of perfumed creams and lotions all laid out on the side in the vain hope that it would make her feel better.

Forty-eight hours to go before she finally left. It seemed like eternity.

Simone got out and rubbed her damp skin with a large fluffy towel, biting worriedly at her lip because she wasn't sure how Jake would react to her today. He had been subdued last night, when Simone had visited him before bed, and she had hardly known how to explain that the day's fiasco didn't mean she wouldn't now be leaving. The poor, confused child had been almost pleased with himself. Simone suspected he had crept back into the hall, seen her embrace with Travis, concluded that things were 'better', 'back to normal'—whatever that was.

She let out a sigh and began dressing. She had done her best to let him down gently, but nothing she said any more, no amount of explanations would make things right for Jake. He only wanted to hear that she was staying.

The Carters had been very understanding; that had been a very small consolation—but a consolation none the less. Simone had phoned and arranged to travel down in a couple of days to begin working straight away for a mutually agreeable trial period.

The weather was dreadful today, matching Simone's mood. A typical English winter's day: splashing persistent rain falling from heavy dark clouds and a bitter wind that cut right through to the bone. She had hoped for brighter, cheerier weather, a chance to get Jake outside in the fresh air, but as it was it looked set in and the day stretched endlessly ahead.

Simone went up to the schoolroom after a lonely breakfast in the kitchen, with just a silent, disapproving Mrs White for company, and tried to think of something exciting to occupy Jake with during the morning. There was everything she could possibly need here, Travis had made sure of that, and after rummaging around in some of the cupboards she came up with a light-hearted idea that maybe, just maybe would succeed in cheering Jake up.

'How about we make some puppets this morning?' Simone suggested brightly, when he appeared a little while later, looking predictably subdued. 'I thought we could use some of the pantomime characters as an idea. You liked Snow White and the dwarfs a lot, didn't you?'

'I liked Sneezy the best,' Jake said quickly, brightening quite perceptively. 'Can I make him?'

Simone's heart lifted steadily throughout the morning as she and Jake worked industriously together, finding suitable bits and pieces, cutting and sticking and generally making a mess.

They were working quietly, sitting on the floor of the schoolroom, rain beating furiously against the window, surrounded by a sea of brightly coloured material scraps, when Travis entered.

Simone heard the quiet click of the door, knew without turning her head that he was in the room, felt the now expected surge of awareness, of pure physical and emotional longing as he moved to the reading corner and lounged against the vivid yellow beanbags.

She made herself look up, just for a moment, just to acknowledge his presence in the normal manner, as if he were just another employer, just another man. It was a mistake, of course. Each time she laid eyes on him, each fresh sighting of the broad frame, the powerful, well muscled body, this morning clad in a dark business suit, left Simone even more weakened, far less able to cope with the cocktail of emotions that assailed every part of her.

'You both look incredibly busy.'

'Do you like my puppet, Travis?' Jake asked cheerfully, holding up a creditable attempt at a dwarf.

'That's brilliant! Well done! You've drawn a very good face. Did Miss Walker help you with that?' Travis drew Jake on to his lap and examined the puppet, which didn't so much look like a dwarf as some sort of grotesque troll, carefully.

'Miss Walker gave me the idea. But I did all this myself!' Jake replied, clearly indignant at his uncle's question.

Travis hid a smile and glanced across towards Simone, who had given in to her resolution minutes before, and was watching him with an intensity that would surely betray her deeper feelings, drinking up every last inch of him, keeping the heart-stopping picture of Travis in her memory for future lonely months and years ahead.

'Where did you find all this?' he asked conversationally, reaching forward to pick up a bundle of material and wool.

'A lot of it was from Mrs White.' Simone wondered if he noticed the slight wobble in her voice, the strain in her throat that talking to him produced. 'She raided her scrap bag.'

'It must be a pretty enormous bag,' Travis commented with a dry smile. 'I've never seen so much stuff!'

'Look at this, Travis! It's like hair. Miss Walker says I can use it to make a monster puppet.' Jake jumped up and grabbed a long, thick skein of black wool, draping it comically over his bright thatch of blond hair, so that it completely covered his face. Giggling, he took it off his own head and laid the wool on Simone's, so that it fell down to her shoulders. 'Hey, Travis! Miss Walker looks funny, doesn't she?'

Simone smiled at Jake, happy that he was back to his usual boisterous self, and then her gaze shifted self-consciously to Travis's face.

What on earth was the matter? Why was he looking at her like that? Simone stiffened, her eyes alert, her mind whizzing. What *was* it?

Narrowed ebony eyes were burning into her face. He was staring, looking at her as if he was seeing something, *someone* for the first time. '*Chantelle*?' His hoarse voice held incredulity, disbelief.

He knew.

There was silence as the tension between them mounted with every passing silent second, heightened somehow by the fact that Jake too had fallen silent, was watching them both with curious puzzlement.

'Travis, why did you call Miss Walker Chantelle? That's not her name!'

Travis shifted his gaze, jerked his head around as if in some kind of daze.

He knew!

Simone found herself trembling at the very thought. He had called her Chantelle almost without hesitation. The black wool—was that what had made him see her, looking like the dyed hair of five years ago? *He had remembered*? She could scarcely believe it. Scarcely take in this vision of him now. She had never seen him like this before—always Travis Steele was in control, on top of any situation, cool and commanding—at the moment he seemed confused, dazed...

'Jake, would you go downstairs and see if Mrs White needs any help with lunch, please?'

Jake pouted, frowning his displeasure. 'But——'

'Just go!' His voice was unusually sharp, making both Simone and Jake jump in surprise. Travis took a controlling breath and then stretched out a hand and fleetingly touched Jake's cheek. 'Please, Jake,' he said more softly. 'I want to have a word with... with Miss Walker in private.

'Take that damned wool off your head!' he commanded savagely, once Jake had reluctantly left the room. 'You look ridiculous!'

Trembling, Simone reached up a shaking hand and snatched the wool away.

'So would you care to tell me,' Travis murmured in a voice that was far too quiet, far too intimidating, 'just what the hell is going on here?'

Simone swallowed painfully, took a breath, swallowed again and then shook her head. 'I... I don't——'

'Don't insult me by being evasive, Simone!' Travis snapped. 'Or should I call you Chantelle? Or perhaps I'd better stick to Miss Walker—that is your real surname, I presume?'

'Please!' Simone placed a frantic hand to her forehead. 'Don't be like this. I——'

'How the hell do you expect me to be?' Travis thundered, rising suddenly from his lounging position on the cushions to prowl around the room like a caged tiger. 'What sort of a sick joke do you think you're playing here?'

'A—a joke?' Simone followed his pacing figure with eyes that showed her own disbelief.

'Don't start sounding so mystified and innocent, Simone.' He turned, surveying her with eyes that held little warmth, a tinge of high colour flaring angrily along each cheekbone. 'It's too late in the day for that now.'

'You can't honestly think I'm here because of a *joke*! You think I'd put myself through this agony, this amount of humiliation for some kind of amusement?'

'So tell me, then!' Travis rounded on her, lancing her with a gaze that made her tremble all over, made the sickness in her stomach reach a level that was almost too much to bear. 'Just what did you hope to gain with this twisted play-acting? Different name, different appearance. What were you doing? Taking bets on how long it would take me to recognise you?'

'You think...you think I planned all this?' Simone breathed incredulously. 'You honestly think I came here with some intention?'

His eyes darkened. 'What the hell am I supposed to think—that this is all a coincidence, an act of fate?' His voice was scathing, each hateful syllable slicing unmercifully into Simone's heart. 'I might have, just might have found that possible to believe if there hadn't been this element of disguise, this deceit!'

'But...but I haven't deceived you!' Simone shook her head. 'I mean...well, not intentionally. That time five years ago... Chantelle, the way I looked, it was just a stupid idea, a challenge... I'd been hurt, insulted. I dressed up that night to prove something to myself.' Simone swallowed, realised she had gabbled in her need to convince him. She cast pleading blue eyes up to the angled planes of his face. 'You've got to believe me, Travis. It wasn't planned.'

There was silence. Then Travis said, 'So why not tell me weeks ago, if this is just some kind of coincidence?'

'I . . . I don't know.'

'That's what was wrong with you on the first morning, wasn't it, when you were in my study? You recognised me instantly, yet you chose to string me along like a fool. You knew we had shared that night, those intimacies and yet you said nothing!' Travis let out a sharp breath and shook his head. 'How could you do that?'

Simone hung her head and tried to think of something, anything to say that would make Travis see how it had been for her, how confusing and shocking. She had made herself hate him over the years because of what she had gone through, the way she had suffered over Katy's death, when in truth he had never been to blame.

'Well, do I get some kind of an explanation or not?' Travis demanded. 'Or are you just going to sit there without a word?'

There was a moment's silence as he moved to the window, hands thrust deep into the pockets of his trousers, staring out at the unceasing rain.

'I . . . I should have left that morning when I recognised you,' Simone whispered numbly. 'I wanted to, but there was Jake and the fact that I've got very little money . . . I had nowhere to go. Then when Jake got so upset . . .' Simone looked up, biting her lip. 'Then I promised to stay . . .' She shook her head inadequately. 'It was such a shock. I could scarcely believe it.' It was all coming out wrong. How could she explain properly, when Travis was so dreadfully angry, so cold and hard and distant?

'So tell me about five years ago,' Travis instructed harshly.

Simone swallowed nervously. 'W-what, exactly?'

'I'd like to know how all that came about. You were a strange mix that night—young and unsure, yet with the look of a seductress.' Travis turned to face Simone, leaning nonchalantly back against the radiator, folding his arms, surveying her with a cool expression of interest. There was a slightly wooden appearance to his features, as if what she was looking at were a mask. Before, Simone realised, just for those few seconds, she had seen the real Travis, the real reaction—that person would probably never be revealed to her again...

She took a deep breath, licking her lips, struggling to assemble her thoughts, her memories, determined to make everything coherent. 'I had never been to a nightclub like that one before. I was unhappy, thinking of leaving. You appeared...' Simone hesitated, felt herself burning up under Travis's suddenly intense gaze. 'When...when you looked at me in the nightclub, showed an interest, I could scarcely believe it.' Simone gave a bleak smile and prayed this agony would all be over very quickly. 'I didn't have much confidence with men and I was so shocked, because I felt like someone else when you looked at me, spoke to me... Look,' Simone added desperately, 'what's the point of going over this? It all happened a long time ago. Surely——?'

'Go on! Tell me,' Travis commanded.

'I found things moving fast, moving in a direction I had never dreamed of before. I was out of my depth. I couldn't handle it.'

'Surely you're not implying I made love to you against your will?' His voice held incredulity.

'No.' Simone shook her head. 'No, I didn't mean it that way...'

His ebony eyes narrowed. 'Are you ashamed of what happened? Is that what this is all about?'

'I was. Or rather I had trained myself to become ashamed. At the time...well, then it seemed right.' Simone's voice fell to little more than a whisper. 'Perfect... Of course, when I woke up next morning and found you had gone...' Simone's voice trailed away miserably as she remembered all over again. 'Let's just say that I came to my senses.'

'I went out early to get some breakfast for us both,' Travis replied in a neutral voice. 'I wasn't much of a housekeeper. I hadn't spent many nights at my London apartment and there was no food in the place at all.' He shrugged. 'I thought it would be nice to share breakfast in bed, so I went to an all-night store.' A muscle jerked beside his mouth as he continued. 'Yes, I found it so easy to forget you, I'd even taken your wretched scarf with me as a memento...'

Simone jerked her head up and stared at him with wide blue eyes. 'You hadn't deserted me?'

He speared her with a look. 'You thought so!'

'I didn't know what to think,' Simone replied angrily. 'Don't look at me like that, accusing me with your eyes! I was so unsure of myself. It seemed natural that you wouldn't want to see me again. I didn't know who you were—I didn't even know your name!' she added bitterly. 'But I knew you were mature, successful, attractive. I knew men like you were used to such experiences.'

Travis shook his head. 'You knew nothing,' he murmured. 'Not a thing! The baby—was it mine?'

The question was blunt, to the point, shocking Simone into stillness. She looked up, twisting the black wool tightly round and round her fingers. 'Yes.'

'You're sure?' His face was white, she noticed, the line of his jaw hard and taut.

'Meaning how many other men did I sleep with?' Simone replied bitterly, feeling anger and misery rising fast. 'I was a virgin, or had you forgotten that small incidental fact, Travis? I know it was a long time ago but——'

'It's possible you slept with someone after me.'

Simone shook her head and scrambled to her feet, her breath coming in short, sharp bursts. 'You can stand there and say that to me!'

She fled from the room, too upset and full of anger to stay in control any longer. Her long graceful legs flew along the corridor, down the sweeping staircase. A moment's pause and then Travis was following. She could feel the determined thud of his footsteps behind as he followed her into the hall and then out into the rain-soaked courtyard.

She made for the wood, running hard, oblivious of the rain and the wind and the dark grey skies. Just anxious for some place away from the house, away from Travis's damnable expression and accusations.

'Leave me alone!' she yelled, when he approached seconds later. His crisp white shirt was damp already, his hair beginning to flatten to his head, glistening and even darker than usual because of the rain.

Simone pressed her hands to her head in a frantic gesture. 'Can't you see I want to be left alone?'

'You can't run away from this one, Simone,' he grated. 'I won't stand by and let you do it!' He came towards her and grasped hold of her arm. She could feel his anger burning through the thin cotton of her blouse. 'Did you honestly expect me to?'

No, she didn't. But she could dream and hope that he would give her at least some time, some space.

'Why didn't you say something? Why deceive me like this for so long?' Travis tipped Simone's chin with firm, uncompromising fingers. 'Have you enjoyed giving me the run-around for these past few weeks, is that it?' he growled. 'Is that what this is all about? You enjoyed enticing me into your bed, allowing me a taste of what it was like to possess you again, knowing full well that once I was snared you would coldly tell me you didn't want to know any more! Was that the plan, Simone?'

'No! No! Travis, please!' Simone tried to tug free from his hold, but he was far too strong, far too angry and determined to let her go so easily. 'It wasn't like that at all, you've got to believe me! I saw you and . . . and it was as if the bottom of my world had dropped away from under me. Five years it took me to piece together my life. After Katy died . . .' Simone's eyes filled with tears, mingling with the rain on her face, and she dragged up a hand to scrub them away. 'After that . . . when I saw you I just didn't know what to do. Can't you understand the turmoil——?'

'You didn't bother to inform me you were pregnant! You had my child,' Travis reminded her needlessly. 'How do you think that makes me feel? Did what we shared that night mean so very little to you?'

Simone gazed up into Travis's angry face, frowning in confusion. 'But . . . but I was just a one-night stand,' she whispered hoarsely. 'I knew that. You knew it.'

'It meant nothing! Is that what you're saying?' Travis demanded, pulling her close against his damp shirt.

'I...I don't know,' Simone began, totally confused by his intense questioning, by this unexpected cross-examination of how she had felt all those years ago. Five years was a long time. Travis would have had untold lovers between then and now...

'You don't *know*!' He ran strong fingers through his wet hair, looked hopelessly up at the dark clouds above his head, then released her suddenly, so that Simone stepped back, stumbling against an exposed tree root.

'I was young,' Simone replied shakily, as Travis instinctively reached out a hand and prevented her from falling. 'I was inexperienced. When I found out I was pregnant I was so frightened.' Simone's voice fell to a whisper. 'I felt so alone and unloved... I blamed myself, I blamed you...'

'Oh, Simone!' Travis pulled her close suddenly, burying his face in her hair. 'I can scarcely believe this is happening. I lost a girl I didn't really know five years ago and felt devastated beyond reason...' He paused. 'When I returned to find you had gone that morning I really couldn't believe it, couldn't believe that I had allowed you to slip through my fingers so easily.'

'I...I don't understand.' Simone pulled away a little, looked up into Travis's damp face, hardly daring to hope. 'What...what are you saying?'

Travis lifted a hand and touched the softness of her lower lip. 'I'm saying I love you, Simone. I'm saying I loved you from that first unforgettable night.'

'You do?' Simone's tone held astonished incredulity and then her mouth broke into a beautiful smile, tears trickled down her cheeks, mingling with the rain. She was fast becoming soaked to the skin, but she didn't care! Travis loved her! She wanted to shout the fact out loud. Travis Steele loved her! Simone threw her arms around his neck. 'Oh, my darling! You don't know how long I've waited for you to say that,' she whispered. 'I love you so much.'

Travis held Simone's face gently in both hands and kissed her mouth with intense erotic passion, sealing their words of loving commitment in a kiss that went on and on and left her trembling with need and desire. When he released her he said softly, 'It may sound hard to believe—indeed I've been convincing myself unsuccessfully for the past five years that it was totally ridiculous to fall in love with someone as quickly and as easily as I did that night—but it is the truth. When I first saw you weeks ago, I was almost relieved, because believe me I've tried, goodness knows how many times, to forget that raven-haired girl who enslaved me, and the instant I laid eyes on you I felt the same spark, the same unexplainable wave of longing to become a part of you, a part of your life. It meant I had got over Chantelle.' Travis shook his head in wonderment, a ghost of a smile on his lips. 'I've been through purgatory and to paradise these last few weeks, struggling with my feelings, having to come to terms with the knowledge that you didn't feel the same way about me. When you didn't turn up at the Carters' household I nearly went out of my mind with worry, do you know that?'

'You have mentioned it,' Simone smiled, placing a hand to Travis's cheek. 'I can't believe this is happening—I can't believe you love me as much as I love you.'

'I do,' he murmured urgently, pulling her even closer to him. 'More than you'll ever know. Will you marry me?'

Simone felt her heart soar and nodded, hastily wiping away the tears that were now flowing with unstoppable speed down her cheeks. 'Oh, yes!'

Travis smiled, kissing the salty wetness from her face. 'You're not supposed to cry, sweetheart,' he teased gently. 'You're supposed to be happy!'

Simone gave a helpless sob. 'I am! Travis, I'm so happy—you'll never know how much.'

Over the next few weeks, he got a pretty good idea.

'So how does it feel to finally be Mrs Steele?' Travis murmured softly, nibbling at a particularly tender place behind Simone's ear. 'Good?'

'Mmm.' Simone smiled up at the ceiling of their honeymoon villa in Tuscany and wriggled, feeling the delicious sensation of Travis's bare skin against her own naked body. 'It feels wonderful, heavenly, beautiful... Shall I go on?'

Travis ran his tongue along the edge of Simone's earlobe. 'If you want to, darling, although I think I've got a pretty good idea already.'

His hand traced a path downwards, his mouth followed, exploring every inch of soft, warm skin.

'Jake likes the Italian maid,' Simone murmured. 'He spent practically all day in the pool. I'm glad we didn't leave him behind. He would have felt so left out, so lonely.'

'He's almost as happy as I am,' Travis replied, pausing in his path of discovery to kiss Simone drowsily on the lips, 'and that's saying something.'

Simone stretched out luxuriously, reaching to touch Travis as intimately as he was touching her, and felt a surge of unashamed pleasure at the look of desire she could so easily produce on her husband's face.

'Hell, Simone! You're gorgeous,' Travis growled huskily. 'Do you know what you're doing to me?'

Simone's mouth widened with a deliberately seductive smile. 'Yes, my darling,' she whispered softly. 'I do.'

Next Month's Romances

Each month you can choose from a wide variety of romance with Mills & Boon. Below are the new titles to look out for next month, why not ask either Mills & Boon Reader Service or your Newsagent to reserve you a copy of the titles you want to buy – just tick the titles you would like and either post to Reader Service or take it to any Newsagent and ask them to order your books.

Please save me the following titles:	Please tick	√
THE WEDDING	Emma Darcy	
LOVE WITHOUT REASON	Alison Fraser	
FIRE IN THE BLOOD	Charlotte Lamb	
GIVE A MAN A BAD NAME	Roberta Leigh	
TRAVELLING LIGHT	Sandra Field	
A HEALING FIRE	Patricia Wilson	
AN OLD ENCHANTMENT	Amanda Browning	
STRANGERS BY DAY	Vanessa Grant	
CONSPIRACY OF LOVE	Stephanie Howard	
FIERY ATTRACTION	Emma Richmond	
RESCUED	Rachel Elliot	
DEFIANT LOVE	Jessica Hart	
BOGUS BRIDE	Elizabeth Duke	
ONE SHINING SUMMER	Quinn Wilder	
TRUST TOO MUCH	Jayne Bauling	
A TRUE MARRIAGE	Lucy Gordon	

If you would like to order these books in addition to your regular subscription from Mills & Boon Reader Service please send £1.80 per title to: Mills & Boon Reader Service, Freepost, P.O. Box 236, Croydon, Surrey, CR9 9EL, quote your Subscriber No:................................ (If applicable) and complete the name and address details below. Alternatively, these books are available from many local Newsagents including W.H.Smith, J.Menzies, Martins and other paperback stockists from 10 September 1993.

Name:..

Address:..

....Post Code:.......................

To Retailer: If you would like to stock M&B books please contact your regular book/magazine wholesaler for details.

You may be mailed with offers from other reputable companies as a result of this application. If you would rather not take advantage of these opportunities please tick box ☐